I've travelled the world twice over,
Met the famous: saints and sinners,
Poets and artists, kings and queens,
Old stars and hopeful beginners,
I've been where no-one's been before,
Learned secrets from writers and cooks
All with one library ticket
To the wonderful world of books.

© JANICE JAMES.

TERRY VENABLES
AND
GORDON WILLIAMS

◆

HAZELL AND THE MENACING JESTER

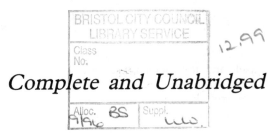

Complete and Unabridged

ULVERSCROFT
Leicester

First published in 1977 by
Penguin Books Limited
London

Originally published under the
pseudonym P. B. Yuill

First Large Print Edition
published 1996
by arrangement with
Penguin Books Limited
London

British Library CIP Data

Venables, Terry
Hazell and the menacing jester.
—Large print ed.—
Ulverscroft large print series: mystery
1. English fiction—20th century
I. Title II. Williams, Gordon, *1934* –
III. Yuill, P. B.
823.9'14 [F]

ISBN 0–7089–3564–8

Published by
F. A. Thorpe (Publishing) Ltd.
Anstey, Leicestershire
Set by Words & Graphics Ltd.
Anstey, Leicestershire
Printed and bound in Great Britain by
T. J. Press (Padstow) Ltd., Padstow, Cornwall

This book is printed on acid-free paper

1

MONEYBAGS BEEVERS and his weird little problem first cropped up on a wet Thursday morning in May. I was just back in the office after flu. Outside it was raining knives and forks. I felt about as merry as him on the slab with the big-toe label.

Needing to be earning I rang a Mr Marshall in Bolton, Lancs, to see about a job he'd mentioned in Eltham, Surrey. It was credit-checking for his wholesale cloth firm, making sure new customers weren't long firm merchants, the kind who trade legitimately until they get big consignments on tick, whereupon they sell off for cash and go missing. Nice work — no knuckledusters and cheques that didn't bounce any higher than a soft-boiled egg.

His secretary said he was in Italy.

I sat there fighting off the day's first fag. My new black brogues were damp. Bargain shoes, always a mistake. Soon as

I got a few quid indoors it was down to Bond Street for a pair of handmades.

The ashtray was still full from last week. It looked revolting. Soon as I got a few quid ahead of the game I'd be puffing six-inch Havanas to go with my St Louis Blues from Bond Street.

Yeah, give me the money and I'll provide the class.

The match almost gave them up for me. It broke on the box. The flaming head bounced off my red sweater on to my lap. I slapped at it but it stuck on, still burning. Give me credit, I stayed as calm as a man with a ferret skipping up his Y-fronts.

The damage came to a slight burn on the sweater, a little black hole in my brown flareds and a black burn on the carpet. British craftsmanship strikes again!

Then the phone rang.

I'd never heard of Philip Beevers but from the off he sounded like we were big mates. He said he'd been recommended by a mutual friend, none other than Paul Shirriff, a smarmy young article who worked for National Security Systems.

He had a warm, throaty voice.

"I've found myself in a very peculiar situation, Jim, I'd like to discuss it with you — today if possible."

"Okay. My office is in Shepherd Market in Mayfair, why don't you — "

"Fact is, Jim old man, I've got a big project coming to the boil and I can't leave my office because I'm expecting a call from Copenhagen — you think I could put you in the picture over a convivial noggin or two? Tonight any good for you? I think you'll find it right up your street, Paul's told me a fair bit about you."

"He tell you my going rate — twenty-five a day plus expenses? Half a hundred in advance?"

"Money won't be any problem — "

"It never is — at the beginning."

"My line of country is just the same, Jim, promises promises and when you come to collect they're tighter than a squirrel with its nuts. Take my word for it you won't be wasting your time. You know a pub called the *Three Colts* up by Drury Lane? Half past six suit you?"

"Okay. How do I spot you among the cocktail set?"

"The cocktail set? Like it, Jim. I'll be wearing a fawn coat with a fur collar, short beard — actually I'll be in a black tie and dicky, I'm taking a few guests to the *Café Royal* boxing. You been to one of these sporting club nights?"

"Nah, I prefer fights out in the open where we can all see 'em."

"I'll take you as my guest sometime, show you what you've been missing. Half past six then?"

"Sure."

"Wonderful, looking forward to meeting you."

I put down the phone. Raindrops battered on the window. Never mind, it was a wonderful world for some, all these bright geezers called Philip Beevers busy copping this London glamour we keep reading about.

There was only one entry in the A to D directory could have been him, *P. Beevers, 34 Inverson Court, Prince Albert Road, N.W.1.* Probably one of those suave blocks looking over Regent's Park, if it was him. I could have buzzed

Paul Shirriff to find out but even thinking about that berk gave me a pain in the part that never sees the sunshine. Every so often he came creeping round and said we ought to go partners and every time I would slag him off. He could eat an insult.

Somebody knocked at the door of the front room. I recognized her small silhouette through the frosted glass. I got up and let her in.

"You didn't tell me you were coming back to work today," said Christine Bunn. "I heard something moving up here, I thought it might be a burglar."

"How're you doing, Titch? I knew it was time to be cured when I started enjoying the all-night taxi-channels on the radio."

"I wish you wouldn't call me Titch. I'm not your kid brother."

"That's true."

We stared at each other across the desk. She had on a green blouse under a sleeveless yellow thing, buttercup colours to go with her complexion. Her blue eyes were as bright as the soap bubbles we used to blow out of wire hoops from

5

Woolworths. Small but lovely. The only trouble was those bright blue eyes always looking to see what I was thinking.

Most of the time I was only thinking ain't life grand but she wanted more than that. Or so I reckoned.

"Fascinating book this," I said, showing her the phone directory, "listen to all these names on the same two pages — Beetz, Beezadhur, Beg Qasim, Begho, Beikens — "

"If you're better could we try that new Japanese restaurant I told you about? I — "

"I'm working tonight. How about Beintema? Beisty? Bekhradnia? Beklik! Bekualac? BELAI AHMED NOOR! Where's the bead curtains and the belly dancers? All we get's bleeding rain. Funny in films, innit, the couple are getting a grip in bed and the camera goes to the window and it's always belting down. Symbolic or what is it? Sinning in the rain? All I get is wet."

"Buy yourself an umbrella."

"A humberella? What would my Mum and Dad say — never mind cousin Tel! Here, my Dad says the weather's

6

changed because they're cutting down forests in Brazil. You think he's gone potty?"

"He must have seen one of those nature programmes on BBC2. Cutting down the rain forests is upsetting the world's ecology."

"I wish I'd been an ecology boy, I'd know all them big words."

She snorted. "Your trouble is you're a walking compendium of all the working-class inhibitions and prejudices — "

"Not *all* of them surely?"

"The problem with your generation — "

"Leave me out! I'm ten years older than you."

"Your age-group then, you were brainwashed into hypocrisy. You think your relationships have to be formalized with wedding-rings and legal contracts. Young people are throwing off these stupid conventions."

"*That*'s why they all look so happy is it?"

"Well — are you happy?"

"If only this bleeding rain would stop I'd be as happy as a pig in shit, if you know what I mean."

She sniffed and pointed at the ashtray. "Yes, I do."

"That's easy mended." I got up and emptied it on the carpet. The mess was horrible. She looked quite shocked. I went to the back room and brought the sweeper. It picked everything up except a couple of obstinate matches.

She shook her head. "I'll have to go back downstairs."

"Just a minute — I got you an executive desk toy as a thank-you present for nursing me." I got it out of the drawer, seven steel balls hanging on a string. You drop one and one pops up at the other end. Drop two and two jump up, clickety-click. "Now you know why dynamic British executives lead the world. If I'm through early tonight I'll ring you, eh?"

She shrugged. She took the toy and went to the door. "Some men buy flowers," she said, "all I get is balls."

The rain went on raining. Mr Marshall didn't ring from Italy. I thought I'd better have a stab at my accounts for the tax man, God rot him.

★ ★ ★

It was twenty past six when I got in the *Three Colts*. I took a stool at the bar, shaking rain off my black and white check jacket and wiping my hands dry on my brown strides. I didn't see anybody present with a fur collar. There was about a score of suavos in the place. Some of them didn't have shirt collars.

It was one of those pubs somebody had once tried to improve with authentic character and atmosphere. You couldn't see the wallpaper for photos of comedians and boxers and singers, all of them autographed to let you know this was the in place for the big stars, only not this year.

The bar was heavy with witty notices. It isn't necessary to be mad to work here but it helps . . .

Complaints have been received about members of the staff dying on the job but refusing to fall down . . .

Eventually I got served. I asked the head warder for half a lager. He was the guvnor actually but he would've been happier swinging a bunch of big keys on

9

a ring. You tell me why the pub trade attracts all these merchants of gloom and sobriety. This one was small and thin with an inch of old doormat under his nose. He was wearing a brown cardigan over a stiff white shirt and regimental tie. Hitler looked jollier on VE night.

"Quiet round here since the Market moved to Nine Elms I expect," I said.

"It still gets bloody busy enough," he growled.

"Sorry to hear that."

He went back to his friends at the other end, a couple of orphan-trappers by the looks of 'em. The next fifteen minutes flashed by at the speed of dry rot.

I never like being in boozers on my Tod Sloan. You always forget to bring a paper to read and you smoke too many just to pass the time. When you're tired wondering who last had a drink from the fancy bottles on the high shelves you watch the other punters and wonder why twits like them are having such a good time. The only nice-looking girl is always with some prize drip but she never seems to want rescuing, generally because she's marrying the creep next morning.

You read all the rubbish in your pockets and check your watch against the bar clock and go over your life twice to see where you went wrong. You read the witty notices again and wonder if some bloke actually makes a living thinking them up.

A couple of stools up from me a fat bloke with watery eyes and a head of hair like seaweed after the oil slick was memorizing every word in the *Evening News*. I tried to see the headlines without actually crawling on to his lap but he was on the financial pages, blubbery lips moving in time with his finger under the lines. It was another bad day for the pound, I managed to read. Must be wearing out, that headline.

At twenty-to-seven something exciting happened. Two laughing Americans stepped in out of the rain, suntanned blokes in black raincoats.

Hitler behind the bar put both hands on the jump, ready to scream that he didn't have a laughing licence, grinning only.

They had a quick look round and decided the rain was better.

Maybe they'd seen the TV commercials for the brewery on the beer handles. You know the one, this shy stranger edges into a crowded saloon bar full of jolly songsters. The barman throws up his arms and bawls, "We're all pals in here — WELCOME!" Three minutes later the shy stranger is playing darts with two enthusiastic blondes who want to have his children.

I went to the carsi. There was no soap but it didn't matter, they'd filed off the hot tap and the cold tap made funny noises instead of water.

"So what's it all about?" I said to this bloke with the fair hair and the damaged nose. He just stared back from the cracked mirror.

Beevers was at the bar when I got back to the funeral party. He was bigger than he'd sounded on the phone, late forties maybe, small pointed beard with a few grey hairs among the brown. The coat was as described, plus a little tweed hat. He had a big nose and sad grey eyes. We knew who we were at a glance. Before we could say much Hitler came up to the bar, smiling for a wonder.

"Hullo, Phil, keeping you busy are they?"

"Mustn't grumble, Ted." He fished under the tail of his coat and came up with a bundle big enough to choke a spindryer. "Know why pound notes are green?" he said. He gave me a wink. "The Jews pick 'em before they're ripe."

"Like it, Phil," chortled Ted Hitler.

"A Jew told me that one," Beevers said, in case I was one of these spoilsports. "Let's take a pew, Jim."

We carried our glasses to a formica-topped table against the wall, the usual kind, four legs all different lengths. He took off his tweed hat and stroked his jet black hair with a white hand that was a lot thinner than the rest of him. The hair was dyed, that inky black with a brown tinge round the edges.

"Sorry about being late, Jim, my Copenhagen call didn't come till six." He looked at his watch, one of those big waterproof jobs that tell you what day it is and how many feet you're drowning at. "I'm pushed for time, Jim, I'll give you the whole story as quick as possible. About two months ago some

13

lunatic started playing practical jokes on us — my wife and me. Nothing serious at first — the complete works of Charles Dickens from a book club, brochures about the Royal Navy and the Prison Service as a career, mail order catalogues — all that garbage you can get from newspaper coupons. Then it got a bit heavier — here, have one of these, a friend brings them in from Jamaica."

I put my fags away and took a short, fat cigar from his case. He lit me from a gas lighter. His nails were professionally manicured. "Good smoke, eh?" he said. "It's not true they're rolled on the thighs of naked Negresses, that's just an old myth."

"What part do they roll 'em on?"

"I like a sense of humour, Jim, I think we'll get on well. Anyway, next we started getting people at the door — insurance reps, mainly Canadian companies — you try getting rid of *them*. Encyclopedia salesmen, central heating salesmen — we even had a bloke with a suitcase full of deaf-aids! they'd all had replies to newspaper ads in my name. Well, I thought it was some of my pals having

14

a joke — let me get you another. Drop of short?"

"Lager's fine."

While Adolf was pouring them he told us another rib-tickler. The bar was a few yards from the table but he had a good carrying voice. "Why did the Arab have the oilfield and the Irishman have the potato field? Because the Irishman got first choice!" He laughed. Any sensitive Micks present must have been in a truce mood. Ted H. hadn't laughed so much since beer went dear. Beevers brought back the drinks. He gave me a weary little grimace, telling me we understood the problems of life unlike all these dumbos.

"You're wondering why I use a dump like this," he said. "I knew Ted in the army, it's handy for my office — anywhere else we'd only have been interrupted by people in my business, I must know hundreds. Where was I? Oh yes, last Wednesday things took a new turn. We had two minicabs we didn't order turning up just after midnight — at the same time! You know what these minicab cowboys are like, I had

15

to threaten them with the polizei before they'd piss off. Then came what decided me I had to take steps. Tuesday night, this week, bloke in a homburg hat turns up downstairs at the desk — we live in a big block — he says he's come to see the deceased and make arrangements *for the funeral*! Some bastard had phoned these undertakers in Camden Town saying he was me — my wife was supposed to have snuffed it. That was just too bloody much. Paul Shirriff is an old mate — I asked him for professional advice and here we are."

"What about the cops?"

He made a sour face and lifted his latest double scotch. "What could they do — even if they bothered?"

"So what do you think I could do?"

"Give me your professional opinion about the chances of nailing this bloody joker and quietly warning him off. You think that's possible?"

"Anybody you can think of who's got the needle to you?"

"Well . . . " he shrugged, "my wife thinks it's the last driver I had. I sacked him just before these hoaxes started,

16

his name was Tony Manders, bit of a hard case. I only had him a month or so, personally I'd class him as more violent than this but as my wife says he does seem an obvious candidate. He wasn't too pleased when I gave him the chop."

"Be very difficult to prove."

He leaned forward. He had a little habit of licking his moustache and beard. He looked successful but not too overjoyed about it. "That's another good reason for not involving the law — we wouldn't have to *prove* it, just satisfy ourselves and then do the necessary — "

"Sorry, I don't break arms."

"Of course you don't. I'm no saint, Jim, but violence isn't part of my code. No, what I'm banking on is the bastard laying off when he knows we're on to him."

"It's your wife sees this chap as the prime candidate — what about you?"

He sighed. "I could give you a lot of bullshit about how popular I am, Jim." He snorted. "I'm very good at bullshit. Jim — I like to think I can sum up people. You're not easily fooled.

Well — the more I think about it the fewer real friends I can name. This rotten hoaxer has really made me look at myself. I never really feel that people like me even when they're being friendly, know what I mean? I know it sounds crazy — I went to a trick-cyclist a few months back, he told me I was insecure! Cost me a hundred and fifty quid all told — to hear what I knew already! If I wasn't insecure I wouldn't be here! I wanted to be *cured*. Ah — not that simple, we don't *cure* you, we let you talk it out and we listen, for twenty-five quid the half-hour."

"Maybe I'm not charging enough."

"Call yourself a psychiatrist and you could be rolling in it, Jim."

"Point is, you got any what you might call proper enemies?"

"I'm beginning to think they're all my bloody enemies. Look, Jim, I don't care what this costs me — "

His hand dived for his hip. I shook my head. "The sight of that bundle could give these dead bodies in here a heart attack, Mr Beevers. I'd only take your dough if I thought I could do a good job for you. Even the cops

18

would be struggling to nail your kind of anonymous hoaxer and I'm just one bloke working on his own. I'd be giving you a lot of fanny if I said I could do anything."

"You won't help me?"

"Not won't — I can't. Straight up."

He nodded sadly. "You're an honest man, Jim, can't be many left. You're probably right. I was hoping you might be a miracle-worker. Oh Christ, look at the time — I must dash."

As we reached the door the King of Fun behind the bar shouted, "Don't do anything I wouldn't do, Phil."

Beevers gave him a wave. As the door closed behind us he said, "Awful little turd, isn't he?"

We said good-bye quickly on the pavement and I trotted to the car. It was belting down. Only twenty past seven. I was hungry but I couldn't face one of Christine's trendy restaurants.

I thought I'd eat first and then call her, maybe go to the pictures. I drove to the fish and chipper in Norfolk Place, just across Praed Street from the big arch into St Mary's Hospital. There

19

was a small queue at the high counter. Being near Paddington Station the tables were mainly occupied by carrot-crunchers waiting for the next choo-choo to the west country, sunny Devon where it rains six days from seven. Ahead of me were a couple of Irish buying something solid to drown in the last ten pints. Geev us a bag o' yer cheeps. Where's de veenagurr?

I lashed in the salt and vinegar and took my haddock and chips outside. The sky had temporarily run out of water. A little bloke in a dark overcoat down to his shins almost fell into me. He was holding on to a big newspaper parcel with both hands. The coat was ripped across the shoulders. White stuff was sticking out, like the flock in mattresses. His trousers were sweeping the pavement behind his heels.

He managed to reach the bus stop, near enough legless but still grabbing on to the parcel. A family of silent Indians or Pakis watched him carefully, three little kids in quilted parkas, the mother in silk trousers and a headscarf, the father in an ordinary Burton's suit. I hoped they thought our weather was worth the journey.

A woman came out of the pub on the corner and yelled something, John or Sean or Ron. Then she shouted a word you couldn't mistake and fell back into the pub. I got in the car and scoffed the fish and chips. People came across Praed Street from the hospital. They got in line at the bus stop, most of them carrying the bags and holdalls they'd taken the grapes in.

They had that look you always see on hospital visitors, glad it's them coming out into the street again but a bit guilty about being glad. I wiped up with a Kleenex and dropped it out the window. I went looking for a phone box.

She wasn't in!

I ended up at the Westbourne Grove ABC seeing *Chinatown* on my tod. Must be comforting, doing your snooping in the Californian sunshine. Ten minutes later I'd forgotten most of it.

Her not being in was a message. My toothbrush was in her bathroom but I wasn't to take her for granted.

I spent the night with my other toothbrush in my own pad in Ravenscourt

21

Park. Great day altogether, hadn't earned a penny and the wet weather was making my dodgy ankle ache.

Maybe I'd sue the bloody match company for the price of new trousers. Maybe. Knowing those bastards I'd be lucky to get the price of a new match.

2

MY mail was one circular addressed to Fitch, the bloke who used to have the office. Did I want a colour illustrated book about forensic pathology at seven nicker?

To a layman the illustrations themselves are far from pleasant.

Just the thing for Mother's Day.

The phone rang. It was the throaty voice of Philip Beevers. He sounded hot and bothered.

"Know what happened last night?"

"Somebody chuck a beer bottle in the ring?"

"The bastard broke into our flat while my wife was having her hair done! He sprayed black paint over about five hundred quid's worth of her clothes! I wanted to ring you last night but you're not in the book."

"Job for the cops now then."

"Jim — I'm at home — could you come over here and have a look at it?

We've got something to go on now, believe me."

There had to be something dodgy about him but that's the case with most clients in this game. And at least this one had plenty of readies, probably more in his hip-pocket than I had in the iron tank.

"Yeah, okay, I'll have a look at it anyway — Inverson Court beside the park, isn't it?"

"How did you know that?"

"Don't take Sherlock Holmes to look in the phone book, Mr Beevers. Give me twenty minutes."

When I went downstairs Christine's door was closed. I didn't try the handle.

The sky over Regent's Park was like the smoke from burning rubber but the rain was holding off. Inverson Court was a medium-sized block near the roundabout before you reach Lord's cricket stadium. It looked very white against the threatening sky. It had balconies and bushes on the penthouse garden, the sort of place where you meet next week's political scandal sliding out the rear entrance in dark glasses.

I swung the Stag down the ramp to the concrete gloom of the basement. There were a dozen or so motors among the big pillars, most of them big shiny jobs, a couple of minis with black windows.

I couldn't see a lift so I went up some concrete steps to a flanged iron door. It wasn't locked. I came out in a gloomy little recess. Round the corner was the foyer. For a moment it felt like a cruise liner, the glass doors to the street, a big mirror covering one wall, easy chairs round a coffee-table with copies of *Vogue* and other intellectual magazines.

Facing the street doors was a sort of cloakroom recess with a counter and a flap. I saw the lift doors and headed past the counter. A man's head came up from behind the counter. He was about fifty, wearing a dark-green uniform jacket with silver epaulettes. His face was a bit red, as if he'd been studying something naughty under the counter.

"Just a sec," he called after me, "are you visiting a resident?"

"Yeah."

"Ah well — you've got to give me your name."

25

"Have I?"

"It's the rules. And who you're visiting."

He liked telling me that. I had him down for a Jobsworth from the start.

"Mr Beevers is expecting me — James Hazell."

He was a biggish bloke, army hairstyle, fair old gut, black hairs sticking out of his noseholes.

"Visitors should use the front door," he said, still making no move to pick up the phone.

"I didn't see any notice, squire," I said, pleasantly enough.

"And parking is strictly reserved for residents unless prior arrangements have been made with this desk."

"How about smoking in bed, squire — do I need to ask the desk about that?"

Like a lot of men with big hooters he preferred to breathe through his mouth. Not quietly, either. Each breath sounded like the last gasp of a dying barrage-balloon. "What name was it?" he growled.

"These ear surgeons do miracles these days I believe."

Silly really but Jobsworths ask for it, traffic wardens, hotel flunkeys, snivel servants, all that sort who don't fancy hard graft themselves but won't let you get on with yours. Ask them to *do* anything the tiniest bit unusual and they always say the same thing — it's more than my job's worth.

He turned his back on me and picked up the phone. I went across and sat at the coffee-table. I had time to read one valuable tip in a glossy magazine. *Geometric Greek boys and judo-loving Japs are replacing Filipino maids as the drudges of the chic.*

I read it twice, trying to fathom it out. It's all down to a proper education I expect.

Jobsworth put down the phone and shouted "Pat!"

Pat appeared from a door at the back of the cloakroom. He was in his twenties, a pale-faced weed with specs that made his eyes twice the size.

He got in the lift with me. He had a green waistcoat over a cream shirt that had seen better days — most of them that week. First man I ever knew who

27

should have had padded shoulders on a waistcoat. His dandruff had a clear drop all the way to the floor.

When the door closed he showed me the interesting colours teeth can run to if you give them the chance. He was from oop north somewhere, where the barmaids eat their young.

"Beevers, is it? You the new driver?"

"Dunno yet. What happened with the last one?"

"Mrs B didn't like him. He were a stroppy bugger — him and George hated the sight of each other — that's George at the desk. I heard Mrs B telling Mr B either Manders went or she'd never get in car again."

"Yeah? The wives is usually the snag — all they think the driver's for is carrying more bleeding parcels."

"Seventh floor, here you go, mate." He put his foot against the door and nodded for me to bend a confidential earhole. He looked both ways, then winked. "Look out for her, mate, bit of a PT expert if you get me. Manders said that's why she didn't like him, he weren't the type to let women mess him about. Only what

28

he said, of course."

"I'll ask her if it's true."

His eyes widened with shock. "Don't you — " then he slumped with relief — "Ee, I thought you was serious for a moment. You almost did my heart an injury. Third door on the left, best of luck."

The corridor had dove-grey wallpaper and green carpeting. The government's little moans about fuel wastage didn't count for much in Inverson Court — the corridor was as warm as a cat's armpit. Number 34 had a shiny black door with a brass knocker in the shape of a lion's head, a peep-hole, a Yale lock, a mortice lock — and a shiny coaching lantern.

A lantern? Inside a block of flats? There's class for you.

I pressed a brass button. There was no sign of the door having been jemmied.

Beevers was wearing a crisp white shirt, dark suit trousers and black leather shoes. His blue silk tie had a gold slide-on pin with a little chain. He looked more like a man in a hotel than at his own front door. "Thanks for coming at such short

29

notice," he said. I had a closer look at the door.

"Doesn't seem to have been forced."

"I'm too shocked to take it all in yet."

I followed him across a square-shaped hall into a long, wide corridor. The first door on the left took us into a lounge with enough floor space for Fred Astaire and Ginger Rogers plus a forty-piece rhumba band tucked in a corner. It was longer than it was wide, with big picture windows and french doors to a balcony. At that height the sky looked even more menacing. He led the way to the other end. Most of the furniture was like the brand-new antiques in a Bond Street showroom.

"Darling, this is Jim Hazell."

She was sitting on a blue velvet sofa with yellow cording round the edges. She looked round and then stood up.

I'd been expecting Beevers to be married to something loud and leathery. She was a bit of a shock.

For openers she was only in her twenties. Her hair was swept back off her face and hung down to her hips.

It was almost white, what they used to call platinum blonde. She had prominent teeth, very milky, and high cheekbones and the kind of skin that reminds you what eggs used to taste like. She was wearing a black sweater with a v-neck, a gold chain round her waist, white slacks, small suede shoes.

We shook hands. My eyes asked the question — what are you doing married to a fat man twice your age? Her light brown eyes held mine long enough to say none of your business.

"Come and see the damage," said Beevers.

The master bedroom was on the other side of the corridor. It was done up mostly in white and gold. The bed was a brass four-poster with white gauze curtains. As a cosy home the Beevers's flat was the kind where you'd need a tie to go to the toilet.

On the white carpet at the end of the bed was a pile of her gear, evening dresses, suits, shiny underwear, tights, stockings, furs, blouses. The top of the pile had been drowned in black paint. A few smears of the same stuff made a

31

trail across the white carpet to an open wardrobe door. Then a line of black ran along the white fitted wardrobes — he'd even gone on spraying across the dressing-table mirror.

"Anything missing?" I said. "Sometimes a burglar will wreck a place if there's nothing worth nicking."

"I have some bits of jewellery in the dressing-table, it's still there." Her voice was well-educated with a slight lisp.

"That's the doing of a deranged personality," Beevers said. I asked if there was any other way into the flat.

"No — well, there's the balcony," he said.

"What about the incinerator chute?" she said sarcastically.

"Don't be silly — this is serious."

She raised her eyebrows. "If it's serious let's call the police." She looked at me. "What can you do?"

"Dunno yet. Let's have a butcher's at the balcony."

He and I stepped out into the wind. There was a table with four chairs, white wrought-iron. I looked over the edge. Seven floors down toy cars moved about in neat straight lines. Across the trees and green spaces of Regent's Park the Post Office tower looked like the top part of a giant aircraft carrier. The obstruction light at the top was a red speck against the black sky. Away to the east the big blocks of the Barbican were white and ghostly.

"Dramatic on a day like this, isn't it?" he said. "Always makes me think London is one huge arena."

"Makes you feel a little like God, does it?"

The balcony was shut off at both ends with thick pebbled glass, wire-reinforced. The glass walls stuck out too far for balcony-hopping. They went up as far as the overhang of the penthouse balcony.

"He could've shinned down a rope," I said. "Who lives up there?"

"A Canadian family — oil. We hardly know them."

"I don't reckon it for a climbing job but you might ask them if they were in all afternoon."

"I'll phone them."

She was standing in the lounge with a big dog, a fancy grey sort with a thin body and long fringes, one of those matching accessory hounds your elegant models go walkies with in the smart parks on Sundays. Beevers got on the phone — one of those real old ones with brass and china fittings. "Jason wants his walk," she said. Beevers put his hand over the mouth-piece. "What can I say — I don't want to tell them about this."

"Say you were expecting a delivery, could it have gone up there by mistake?" I said. He nodded eagerly. He didn't seem any too bright to have earned all this. "Jason wants his walk," she said again. She was wearing a new sheepskin coat, very white and yellow. Beevers looked nervously from her to me and back again. "Jim probably wants to ask some questions — oh, hallo, Mrs Galbraith? It's Beevers here from down below — "

She and I stared at each other while he was talking. She didn't smile. Maybe she was tired of eyes asking why *him*. He put the phone down. "No, they were in the whole day."

"Who would know you were getting

your hair done?" I asked. She shrugged. Jason yawned. "Simone always has her hair done on a Thursday afternoon, don't you, darling?"

She nodded. The darling sounded forced, as if he had to remind her whose side she was on.

"You got a cleaning woman or what?"

"Mrs O'Brien, she only comes in the mornings. She has Fridays off."

"How long were you out?"

"Oh — from about half past two till just after seven."

"Mrs O'Brien — she got keys?"

"She didn't have anything to do with it! I've had her for four years, we're friends — I give her clothes and things."

"How about Rin Tin Tin there — good watchdog?"

I knew she wouldn't like that. "I always take Jason with me," she snapped. "Is that all?"

"Anybody see you leave the building? The desk blokes? Neighbours?"

She laughed at my stupidity.

"You don't really have neighbours in the normal sense in a place like this," he said tactfully. What would a common herbert like me know about suave living? "The next flat along belongs to some Arabs, we never see them much — down the hall there's a Mrs Temperley-Drabble, she's not the neighbourly kind — "

"You're saying nobody saw you go out?" She blushed angrily.

"The porters saw me," she said, "if I'd known it was to be so important I would have asked them to punch my card."

"There wouldn't be enough punch between the pair of them," I said. She knew exactly where I was at. She managed to look insulted and flattered at the same time. "Yeah, okay then, your husband can fill me in about the rest of it."

He pecked at a cheek that didn't exactly offer itself. "When Jim is through I'll go straight to the office," he said. "Shall I shift that mess in the bedroom?"

"No, leave it," was her command, "I'll sort out what can be saved."

"Might salvage some items for Mrs O'Brien," I said. She gave me a look that would have withered an iron bush and went off with the hound. They made a handsome couple. Beevers flopped down on a blue velvet chair. His tongue was busy making sure his beard hadn't fallen off.

"Pretty obvious he had keys to get in here," I said. "How many keys are in existence?"

"I'm not sure about the Yale but I had the other lock put in last year — there're only four keys for it, one for Simone, one for myself, one for Mrs O'Brien and one I keep at the office just in case."

"Either of you lost any keys lately?"

"Not that I know of."

"This Mrs O'Brien — what's she like?"

"Thick as a docker's sandwich but honest I'd say."

"She got a family?"

"Her husband's dead, she's got three small kids — I see what you're thinking, no, the oldest is only nine or ten. What do you honestly think, Jim?"

"You better face it, Mr Beevers, that isn't just a joker you got on your back, that's an authentic enemy."

He nodded slowly. He went on looking at me. The only noise in the lounge was the faint creaking of wind massaging the windows. For a moment it felt like we were two dummies in a showroom window.

"My guess is it's somebody who knows you pretty well. What kind of character was this driver you mentioned?"

He took a deep breath. "Simone thinks it's Manders," he said, "I think it's just possible it was the driver I had before Manders. I had to sack him for drinking. At least, I did think it might be him till last night. Look, Jim, before I say too much — are you going to handle this for me?"

What should I have done? Disappointed the man?

I was still hurting from working for a sad widow who conned me into thinking she was broke. I'd given her widow's rates and then she turned out to be bleeding loaded.

Only this client was practically gasping to shove readies in my face.

What should I have done? Sent him to the Citizens' Advice Bureau?

"Yeah, okay," I said. "Only I got to warn you, Mr Beevers — "

He let out a big sigh, waving his arm

at me. "I'm so relieved, Jim, I can't tell you." He stood up. "I need a drink. You?"

"Bit early for me thanks."

He went across the room to an antique chest. His backside was wider than his shoulders. I could see the bulge in his hip-pocket. Maybe he enjoyed dishing it out. Why the hell should I feel guilty? He had to have a good reason for not wanting the cops in.

"Funny," I said, "both these capers were directed against your wife. It was her supposed to be dead and now it's her gear he's slaughtered."

He looked back at me from the genuine antique cocktail cabinet. I got a fag in my mouth and wondered if the lump of brown marble with the hollow in the middle was an ashtray or an empty paddling pool. I put the match back in the box in case it was modern art.

"That did occur to me," he said. "This could be on the delicate side."

"If I'm taking your money there's only one thing you've got to remember, Mr Beevers. I'm working for you, nobody else. And you've got to trust me, know

39

what I mean? I know private detectives have a lousy reputation — "

"Paul Shirriff told me all — "

"Shirriff don't know enough about me for his opinion to count, Mr Beevers."

He sat on the sofa, a cut-crystal glass in his thin white hand. "I've been around, Jim, I think I ought to have some sixth sense about who to trust by now."

"Maybe. Maybe you haven't seriously thought about all the angles to this. For starters — this is the delicate bit — how are things between you and your wife?"

He blinked at that. "How do you mean?"

"As I say, Mr Beevers, you've got an enemy — or she has. You're asking me to turn him up. Maybe what I come up with won't be good news."

"But you don't think — "

"It's early days, Mr Beevers, I'm only considering all possible angles."

"Of course. As you can see, there's an age difference but otherwise we're just like any normal married couple, not all sweetness and light but who is?"

He crossed his fat thighs and stared sideways out of the big windows. I saw an ashtray on a low table at the other end of the sofa. Also on the table was a china leopard, about lifesize. It had very realistic eyes. In the corner beyond the big carved fireplace was a colour TV with cute little shutter doors to hide the vulgar screen when suavos dropped round for witty chat and After Eight mints. One thing was for sure, he wasn't running all this on thirty bob a week.

I took the ashtray back to my chair. "I see what you mean," he said, hesitating a bit. "I don't know much about your profession — would you feel obliged to tell the police if you heard about a crime?"

"Depends I suppose. If it was murder — I'd have to, wouldn't I? Drugs — I think anybody dealing in drugs is entitled to have his arms chopped off. Anything else — I'd have to see how it affected me personally."

He hardly listened. He'd already decided to trust me anyway. "My previous driver, Bert Thornton, he owes me a bad turn. He ran a man down in Leicester Square one night in December. It was pretty late and pouring down, bloke steps out from between the parked cars round the gardens in the middle — we went smack into him, no chance." He took a deep breath and let it out with a shudder. "I was late for a supper party in the Savoy, I made Bert keep going, nobody had seen it, the bloke was flung back between the parked cars, there weren't many people on the pavement — some wino I thought, probably too pissed to feel it. Bert was in a terrible state — I was shouting at him to keep going — then next day it was in the papers, he wasn't a bum, he was an area sales manager from Kent — wife, three kids, great future ahead of him . . . oh my God . . . "

"Wiped him out?"

"Oh yes. Fractured skull. Must've been a couple of hours before anybody found him. Bert was destroyed. Never had a black mark in thirty-five years' driving. He started drinking — nerves I suppose. I held on to him as long as humanly possible but in the end — mind you, I saw him all right for money and I told him to come to me any time — of course I was more to blame than him." He shut his eyes and shook his

42

head. "If you knew how often — still, too late now. Anyway, that's why I couldn't call in the police. As soon as they started questioning Bert about the hoaxes he was bound to tell them about the hit and run — I wasn't worried for myself, believe me — if anything I'd be half-relieved to be punished — it was Bert I was thinking of. Hit and run? Manslaughter? They would have charged him with something, wouldn't they?"

"You say you saw him all right?"

"I gave him five grand in cash. By the way, my wife doesn't know about that, only Bert and me."

"Lot of readies to have laying around, innit?"

"My business is like that."

"What is your business exactly, Mr Beevers?"

"I have quite a number of interests actually. My basic line is furniture — importing special lines from Scandinavia. Then I diversified. I have an associate in a music agency, Lou Nicholas is his name, we've been dabbling in various things — open-air festivals among others, some successful, some not. Money is very tight this year."

"You mean there's years when it isn't? Did Thornton get another job?"

"Nobody's asked me for a reference."

"What about this Manders bloke?"

"I had him for about two months. Simone never liked him. She said he was always making hints — you know, lovely young wife, middle-aged husband, strapping young driver. He was about the most aggressive person I've ever known — his very manner made you feel threatened."

"How did he take it when you gave him the chop?"

"He wasn't pleased."

"How old are these two blokes?"

"Bert's fifty-five, fifty-six. I had him about five years, always been a driver. Manders was twenty-eight. I got him through an ad in the *Standard*. He'd been driving a minicab. He'd been in the army for five years, clean discharge, all that sort of thing."

"Live in, did he?"

"We're not as grand as that. He had a place in Adelaide Road, just up the road a bit in Swiss Cottage."

"They have keys to the flat?"

"No, only for the car. Of course they would sometimes have my keys — they're all on the same ring, they could've been copied."

"Okay. So we've got two blokes with some kind of reason, they both had access to your keys, they both know the layout, they'd both know your wife's routine. How about your office? Sacked anyone there lately?"

He looked hurt. "I don't make a habit of it, Jim."

"Business enemies?"

"What else?" He gave me a weary smile. "I know a lot of people but whether they like me or not — you know how it is, Jim, when things are going well you think the world's a friendly place but . . . "

"Things not going too well are they?"

"Up and down. I should never have gone into the agency business. I had delusions of making a big success in something more glamorous than furniture."

"Mr Beevers, this is either being done

for revenge or for money. You haven't had any notes or phone calls asking for dough so it looks more like revenge. Once I start digging I could easily blunder into something that might embarrass you, unless I know in advance."

He shook his head.

"If I could give you an example, Mr Beevers," I said, trying to be patient. "I used to work for a firm that handled a lot of industrial stuff. One of the clients was a big building contractor up in Birmingham, he thought one of his staff was getting bunged by the opposition to leak them details of his tenders for council jobs. We nailed the geezer all right — only he got so riled he grassed to the Inland Revenue about how our client was dodging tax in a big way. They both ended up doing bird — you know, porridge, stir — prison, Mr Beevers. See what I'm getting at?"

He stared me straight in the eye. "I've fiddled my tax with the best of 'em, Jim, but I don't have any skeletons in the cupboard."

"That's what Christie told the borough health inspector and he had a corpse in every room. Plus one or two in the garden." He looked hurt.

"If I knew I'd tell you, Jim, honestly."

"Okay. I'll start with Thornton and Manders if you give me their addresses — and the name of the funeral geezer."

"That's wonderful, Jim." His right hand came out of his hip-pocket with the big bundle. The strain of jacking up his big end made him pant a bit. He looked about as healthy as a flat tyre. How was his heart standing the strain of keeping her happy? Or did he keep her happy? Or did I just have a low mind?

He thumbed five brown ones off the outside of the bundle, half a hundred, didn't even make a dent in it.

"You'd better send a letter to my office address saying you're retaining my services," I said. "You don't have to say for what or how much."

"It won't show on my books, Jim, forget it as far as the tax is concerned."

"I got to show the bastards something or they get suspicious."

It took him ten minutes to get ready. He kept forgetting things and then finding them and then forgetting which skyrocket he'd put them in. His chat was the usual stuff. London's thick with geezers like him, middle-aged flash harrys who didn't quite finish the elocution lessons. They always have a bale of readies for impressing you but you're never too sure how they made it in the first place. They're always on the edge of big deals and they can tell you ten tricky ways of koshering bent money through moody companies in Gibraltar — surely we've all got bent money that needs a false birth certificate?

One thing I've learned about that sort — all the stock is usually in the window.

As he locked the door he looked at me with a sad face. "Got a family, Jim?"

"Divorced. You'd better tell these geezers at the desk I'm working for you but don't say what at. Let them think I'm your new driver if they want."

"Whatever you say."

"How come all these salesmen got up to your flat anyway? He nabbed me quick enough."

"I had a quiet word with George after these things started, he's double-checking on all callers."

"Do they know about the paint job?"

"No! Christ, if the other tenants hear I've been broken into and haven't called the police I'd be as popular as pox."

In the lift going down Pat of the missing shoulders said, "Like me to wash your car tonight, Mr B?"

"Be obliged, Pat," said Beevers. His right hand did the journey it knew best. Pat got a oncer off the bundle. It disappeared into his waistcoat with as much noise as a goldfish saying good night.

In the foyer Jobsworth said, "Looks like we're due for a downpour, Mr B."

"Shocking weather, George," said Beevers. "By the way, this is Jim Hazell, he's working for me now so let him up any time."

"Very good, Mr B," said the big flunkey. It wasn't quite enough to earn a nicker off the bundle. I gave him a friendly wink. From the look I got I took it we were never going fishing together. Beevers went on across the foyer into the little gloomy alcove, round the corner from the desk.

"Any stairs in this place?" I asked.

He showed me another door facing the door down to the basement. "It's got bars on the inside," he said, "it only opens one way, nobody ever uses it except for furniture removals." I tried but it wouldn't give. We went down into the basement. Our heels cracked on concrete. Our voices had a slight echo. The parked cars looked like dead objects from busier days.

"You get no insurance on the damaged clothes if you don't report it to the cops," I said. Beevers licked his moustache.

"That's the least of my worries, Jim. Between you and me, Simone can spend that much in a week. You know that joke — the man whose credit card was stolen? He didn't bother to report it because the thief was spending less than his wife." Then he did a funny thing. He put his thin, white hand on my sleeve. "Do the very best you can for me, won't you, Jim? My life's got enough problems as it is. You'll find me very grateful."

Then he walked away quickly. The

Rolls was at the far end, in the shadows behind a pillar. I got in the Stag. He gave me a little wave as he slid past, a big man in a big car.

I came up the ramp into the daylight brand of gloom and crossed the road. I pulled into the kerb and switched off. I didn't have time to light a fag before she came along the pavement from the park, the fashion hound high-stepping beside her. Her white-blonde hair and yellow sheepskin coat made her look like something that had wandered into our dreary world from a Technicolor film. I got out before she could cross the road.

"Your husband's just gone, Mrs Beevers. There's a couple of things — "

"What sort of things?"

"Bit chilly out here — like to sit in my car?"

"No thank you."

"If you'd rather go upstairs — "

"This is as cosy as I prefer to be."

"When you went out to the hairdressers' — did you definitely lock both locks?"

"I always do."

"Mrs Beevers, your husband's told me to handle this the way I see best. Trouble is, once I start sniffing about no knowing what'll turn up, do you?"

She began to look angry. "What does that mean?" The lisp was more noticeable when she was excited, I noticed. Quite attractive, too. On a woman anyway.

"As I told your husband, Mrs Beevers, could be this joker's got the needle to you and not your husband. It might save red faces later — you got anybody who maybe hates you that bad, maybe somebody your husband don't know about?"

Get your face slapped here, Jim me old son. She stared at me. The hound was too well-bred to sneer but it shook a haughty fringe or two.

"I'll give you the benefit of the doubt and assume you're trying to be tactful. I have no secrets from my husband."

"There wasn't any kind of note or message beside the clothes?"

"There was not. Are you suggesting — "

"This is a job to me, Mrs Beevers, I'm getting paid a pony a day to stop these things happening, that's all. It don't worry me none if you're at it with two milkmen. I'm not saying you are, I'm considering all possible angles.

Okay? This Manders bloke — if it's him and I nab him he's liable to throw all kinds of shit — beg your pardon, make up lies and smear. Be as well if I had a clue about what to expect."

She actually came near to smiling. At least her nostrils expanded a fraction. Her big front teeth were very white. "He wasn't screwing me if that's what you're inferring. He may say he was, he certainly wanted to. If he does, please tell Philip. Good-bye."

They went across the street together, a handsome couple with fine pedigrees. "You lucky dog," I muttered, getting into the car.

I got out a fag and then put it away and headed off under the nasty sky for a body shop in Camden Town. ❦

3

IT was next door to an Indian restaurant in a turning off Camden High Street, *E. Waugh and Son, Funeral Directors*. They had a couple of plain brown vases against fawn curtains in the window.

Like the old Frankie Howerd joke, what does a vet who specializes in ravaging tomcats use for a window display?

I don't know what I expected but I didn't steam in and yell SHOP!

The girl got up from her electric typewriter. She was plump, about thirty-five, a brown dress with a white collar, no wedding-ring. Her face knew how to show sympathy.

"Can I help you, sir?"

I don't know why I felt so spooky, I've seen plenty of dead ones in my time. I killed a bloke once. Every time the sun shines I think he still ought to be enjoying it. Hardly a day passes but I wish I hadn't done for him.

"My name's James Hazell, I'm working for a Mr Philip Beevers," I said. Then I wondered why I was speaking in a hush. "One of your chaps went to see Mr Beevers on Tuesday night — Prince Albert Road — there was a hoax call."

"Oh yes — it must have been very distressing for them. It was Mr Albert actually. Would you like to speak to him?"

"Who took the call?"

"I did, actually, but Mr Albert really ought to know you're here."

She went through the door at the back. All I saw was more fawn curtains. She came back with a stocky man in a crisp white shirt. He had thick shoulders and ruddy cheeks and a few shiny strands going across a shiny skull. His hands were brown and exceptionally clean.

I told him what it was all about. "Miss Bragg took the call," he said. "Tell Mr Hazell what he wants to know, Molly. Here — has my dear father rung in yet?"

"No." He went tut-tut. "Getting old, that's his trouble, can't take his beer no more." He looked at me with a serious face. "Ever seen backstage in one of these?"

"I haven't as it happens."

"Come through when you're finished with Molly, I'm a great believer in dispelling the mists of ignorance and fear."

"I didn't know it showed."

He winked and went back through into the mysterious part. Miss Bragg remembered the call quite well. A man's voice, twenties or thirties maybe. He'd said his wife had just died and he wanted her cremated at Golders Green. It was about four in the afternoon. She took the address and asked if he had the doctor's certificate and if his wife belonged to any religion. Just routine. He said his wife would've liked a Church of England service. She didn't remember any particular speech mannerisms — fairly educated she would have said. They got the occasional moody call, mostly from schoolkids, she reckoned to spot a hoaxer because kosher calls came from a friend or relative who was trying to be business-like, whereas fake callers were often a bit hysterical. If she had any doubts she always got a number to check back.

"Mr Albert was going up to Hampstead so he said he'd drop in," she said. "The man was so natural-sounding it never entered my head he was a hoaxer."

"Posh was he — Oxford accent and that?"

"Well, middle-class, you know."

"Ai can doo a reely naice accent when Ai try."

She smiled. "You sound like Charlie Drake the comedian when he's trying to be posh. Funny, just talking about it I'm remembering things — he said she'd died suddenly from a cerebral haemorrhage — only twenty-eight."

"He definitely said twenty-eight?"

"Yes. I remember thinking how brave he was being about it."

"Deep voice or what?"

"Medium — normal."

"Did he say why he picked your firm?"

"That's right — he said we'd handled a funeral for friends of his in Islington."

"Didn't say which funeral?"

"No — and we do an awful lot in this

whole area. Am I being any help to you
— I'm sorry I can't — "

"No, great help, thanks a lot."

"I think Mr Albert's waiting for
you — "

"Oh. Serious was he?"

"As serious as he ever is."

"He'll be the cheeriest one in there I
expect."

What did I see? A range of coffins at
various prices and a little side room done
up as a chapel. Not a whatsit in sight.
Mr Albert enjoyed watching my face.

"Expecting to see the shelves groaning
under the weight of customers were you,
old chap? Mostly we lay 'em out in their
own homes — if they don't have a spare
room we have to bring 'em here for the
necessary, embalming and such — pity
I couldn't give you a demo. Anything
wrong, old chap?"

"I suppose you'd get used to it in
time."

"The doctor has 'em when they're
warm, we get 'em when they're cold."
He gave me a nudge. "Only a degree
or two of difference." He snorted at
his own wit. "Been at it since I was

fourteen, old chap. Tell you one thing — it's a good steady living." He gave me another dig. His face stayed straight the whole time. "No slumps in this racket. My old man started round about the first war, down the street a bit, cor, they had real send-offs in those days — often they didn't have money to feed themselves but there was always a bit put by for a proper send-off, must've been lovely in those days, horses they used to have, all done up, shiny harnesses — only touch of class some of them had in their whole lives." He raised his eyebrows and gave me a wink. Cheery sort of devil he was. "Miss Bragg give you everything you needed? Nasty business for those people — " the elbow again — "been nastier if it hadn't been a hoax, eh? I'll bet most of 'em do wish it were a practical joke when they see me at the door. Get Molly to give you one of our cards — never know, do you?"

"I'm hoping for a few years yet."

"Bloke in your line, getting about the town, solving murders and so forth, maybe put some business our way, eh?" Another nudge. "Why so solemn, old chap, isn't death just Nature's way of telling you to slow down?"

★ ★ ★

Adelaide Road is the sort of street that makes a born Londoner feel he's a stranger. You speak with your normal Hobson's choice and they say beg votre pardon, foreigners and students and such, you know, university degrees and mouldy clothes.

It was a tall terraced house. The door was shabby and there was a bare hole where the letterbox used to be. Manders didn't appear on any of the cards so I kicked off at the bottom. The fourth bell got feet moving inside. Somewhere a typewriter was clacking away busily. An intellectual preparing to tell the world about his innermost anxieties I expect.

A tall woman opened the door. She was in a brown jumper and bleached jeans tucked into high black boots. Her hair was up in a ponytail. She was about forty, with red hands and no make-up. Well-built, too.

"Sorry to trouble you," I said with

my pleasant-chap's smile. People like that usually reckon any born Londoner they hear must be a thief or a hooligan. "I'm looking for somebody called Tony Manders who lives here, he isn't on the board."

"I can't say I know the name," she said. She sounded like an army colonel. In the hall there was a table with a lot of unclaimed mail. Next to the table was a dingy pram. The whole place needed spring-cleaning, with a flame-thrower.

"He's a biggish chap, about twenty-eight, dark hair, works as a driver or showfer."

"Oh yes! I know who that is. Of course. He lives on the third floor, I often saw him in his shafoor's cap. I think his wife is in — " she gave me a grimace — "they live together anyway."

She stepped past and peered at the buttons. The boots had highish heels. The way she strode about she looked ready to leap into a wild cossack dancing. "There you are, Sillitoe, number nine."

"Thanks, I'll give it a buzz."

"I shouldn't bother — go straight up, if the pram's here she's here."

I followed her in. One thing about the educated, they love shopping each other. If a stranger comes round with a lot of whys and wheres in the East End or Fulham or Shepherd's Bush or any normal place nobody knows from nothing about anything — it's second nature, the busy stranger is always the enemy. Even if you hate the bloke upstairs you don't grass on him because he's one of yer own.

Your educated now, they're taught early on to shop everybody for the good of society. I expect it makes sense if it's your society.

The big lady in the high boots left me on the first landing. The stair carpet was showing thread in the places where it wasn't slippy. Some of the doors were painted with big flowers and Mickey Mouse signs. One had a metal sign nicked from the City of Westminster — *Gentlemen*. Hard to tell if it was a description or an invitation.

Number nine was on the third floor. A small girl opened the door. She was wearing jeans with daisies sewn on the knees and a white blouse with puffy sleeves. Her hair was parted in the middle and hung down her face like curtains. She had a black eye going yellow and a swollen lip. Her face was deadly pale with a few spots on the chin.

"Sorry to trouble you, luv, is this where Tony Manders lives?"

"Not any more. Who are you — one of his friends?" She sounded like an ordinary Londoner but that was a bit hard to believe in Adelaide Road. Maybe she was an Australian with ambitions.

"My name's James Hazell, I'd like to see him about a personal matter. Gone has he?"

"Is he in trouble?"

I had on my Aberdeen face, the one that gives nothing away. "No, I'd like a chat with him, that's all."

"It is trouble, I can tell. Come in."

There wasn't a carpet in the place. Bare wood. The walls were covered with paintings. Some were on bits of wood, some on squares of cardboard. They were all much the same, a naked woman with a baby surrounded by jungle. The colours were mainly dark browns and purples, except for the woman and the kid, who

63

were always bright yellow.

In the front room there was a low divan bed, no blankets, just one of those continental quilt jobs. The furniture was mostly orange boxes covered with cheesecloth.

In the middle of the room was a table with one wooden chair. The table was spread with newspapers. The papers were smeared with paint.

One corner of the room looked a bit like an altar. There was a basket-work cot stuck into the corner at an angle. It was decked out in white cloth, little curtains round the legs, another lot of curtains hanging from the hood.

Two stretches of the same white cloth were pinned to the floor. They came up to the top of the hood. There they were tied in a big bow, like the front of the bride's car.

"Are you from the police?"

"No. You expecting them?"

"I think it's all wrong that a man can hit a woman and bash her up and they won't take action because it's only a domestic incident." She was standing between me and the cot. I didn't see anything I would've risked sitting on.

"Manders give you the shiner, did he?"

"Yes." She shook her head and pulled her hair behind her ears. She gave me an old-fashioned look. "Why do you want to see Tony?"

"Just a chat about a personal matter. Any idea where he can be got?"

"Tell me why you're looking for him."

I got out my fags.

"Would you mind not smoking?" she said quickly. "I never let anyone smoke near Duffy." I took it Duffy was in the cot. He wasn't moving about much.

"I'm an inquiry agent," I said, putting away the fags. "Manders might be able to help me. What kind of bloke is he?"

"I wish I'd never met him. I was very naïve then, I wasn't into meditation or *anything*. He's full of charm when he wants to be but a lot of psychopaths are like that, aren't they? Do you think it can be passed on?"

"Beg your pardon?"

"Duffy is Tony's son." She walked across to the cot. She leaned over the white streamer to peer in between the cloth curtains. She came back to the other side of the table. "You're very quiet but your vibrations are extremely aggressive," she said. "You're very dangerous, aren't you?"

"Me? Nah, all I want is to ask him a few things — "

"Are you a gangster?"

I had to laugh. "No, I'm self-employed."

"Is there any chance he *could* go to gaol?"

"You'd like him sent down, would you?"

"He beats me up every time he gets the chance. I don't want him ever coming near Duffy again."

"Living together were you?"

"Yes, for six months. Violence and sex are the only ways he can express himself. I was totally unaware when I met him, I hadn't even begun to relate. It's our only hope, isn't it?"

"Too true."

"If I told you where he works would you tell him I told you?"

"Not if you don't want me to."

"People like you frighten me. Very

few men are brave enough to discover themselves, actually."

"It's Manders I want to discover. I'll not breathe a dicky-bird about you."

"Your sacred promise?"

"Boy Scout's honour, cross my heart and hope to die."

"He left this last week," she said, lifting the paint-smeared newspaper on the table. It was a card, *Excelsior Taxi Service, Day and Night*, no address, just a 734 number, the old Regent exchange in the West End.

"Thanks a lot. Listen, you ever see him cutting up newspapers or magazines?"

"No, he only ever read pin-up magazines."

"You ever hear him mentioning the name Beevers?"

"That was the businessman he used to work for. He left that job because the man's wife treated him like dirt — at least that's what he said. He probably tried to seduce her, knowing Tony, and she wouldn't have it. He's a compulsive womanizer you know."

"Tuts tuts."

"Being a man you probably go in for

the same ego satisfactions." All the time we were talking she stood between me and the baby. She had all the trendy ideas, men were destructive, society was polluting itself to death, our food was poisoned, war was coming in two minutes and our only hope was to kneel in front of hairy gurus from caves in India and find inner harmony.

"I read in the papers that this latest guru went to California and bought himself two mansions," I said. She tightened her face. "You got a photo of Tony by any chance?"

"No, I never take photographs, I agree with the Indians, taking a photograph steals a part of your soul."

"Must be tough on all them Apaches in the cowboy films. How was Tony on all this inner harmony?"

She shrugged. Her hair had worked loose from her ears. Only her nose was keeping it from meeting in the middle. "Tony is a philistine fascist with no interest except self-gratification. I'm so worried Duffy turns out like him — I don't think he will, though, a baby can sense whether its mother has inner harmony — I feed him myself, of course."

"Who else? What does Tony look like would you say?"

"Do you know Elvis Presley?"

"Only by sight."

"Tony models himself on Elvis Presley. He thinks he looks like him. He doesn't but he does his hair the same way — all that horrible grease!"

"Sounds like a real winner all round."

"He's a monster! There was some officer he didn't like in the army, he was always saying one day he'd get into Tony's cab and he'd take him somewhere quiet and beat him up. Or track him down with a gun and kill him."

"Can't wait to meet him. Anyway, thanks for helping me — I won't mention your name."

She went first to the door. Her bare heels were hard and cracked but fairly clean.

"It won't matter next week," she said. "I'm leaving here to join a group in Gloucestershire, we grow our own food and study Nature, really we're rediscovering our own identities, of course."

"Of course. Don't mind me asking but these paintings — not that I know anything about art or that — but they're all the same, aren't they?"

"Madonna and child, it's my major theme. The style is intentionally primitive. They're meant to be like early Russian ikons."

"I see."

She was a short little thing and to take one off the wall she got up on her toes. Her blouse pulled up from her jeans while she was dragging out the pins. There was a yellow bruise on her soft white back.

"You can have this one," she said. It was a square of cardboard, yellow mum and kid in a purple forest.

"Oh. Are you sure?"

"I like giving them to people."

"Thanks, I'll put it up in my office. Cheers."

She closed the door. I thought I heard the baby crying.

I went down the slippery stairs with the cardboard painting under my arm, black side facing out in case anybody sussed me for an art thief.

It was only just after two. The sky was so dark it felt as if something dramatic was going to happen any minute. The end of the world maybe.

I thought I'd better get some grub inside of me before I caught up with Tony Manders, popular maniac-about-town.

4

AN hour later I was heading up Shaftesbury Avenue. My feet felt dry for the first time in days. I had a mixed grill inside me and Beever's five tenners in my back pocket. With a bit of luck I'd hit on Manders first time out and wrap the job up in one day. Nothing could be finer in the state of semolina.

Among the crowds I spotted a well-known actor from television, a tall bloke with sandy hair, always plays the treacherous toff who sneers at everybody. Can't think of his name. He was wearing a blue denim suit, pale suede boots and a nice new tan. He looked at us all to see if we were recognizing him.

Behind him came a busker with a harmonica and a flat cardboard box, a burly geezer with red flaking skin. Instead of waiting for people to bung in the nobbins he was choosing victims and dancing along the pavement in front of them — backwards. He did his little skips and tooted his harmonica and waved his box at them. They had to pay to get shot of him. It looked like harder work than sneering on television.

The pavements were thick with people in good clothes looking for new things to buy but according to the newspaper bills the times were diabolical. Fares were up. Petrol was up. Electricity was going up shortly. Every bleeding thing was going up except the one that matters.

Excelsior Minicabs was halfway down a side-street on the south side of Shaftesbury Avenue. The entrance was between a drum shop and a Chinese grocery. The drum shop was full of kids picking the gear that would make them as famous as The Beatles.

The Beatles? How old-fashioned. It's the Heavy Metal Kids today, according to the posters. Anybody want to buy a Marvin Rainwater record?

There was nothing on the ground floor, just a narrow hallway and stairs. I was just starting to climb when a youngish spade in a leather jacket and floppy velvet cap came trotting down. I moved to one side.

73

"You lookin' for a cab, chief?" he said. He didn't have a beard exactly, just a few long hairs sprouting under his bottom lip.

"Office upstairs is it?"

"I'll take you, save you climbin' all the way up. Come on, I got my motor in Gerrard Street."

I followed him out on to the pavement. I thought I saw a clever way of getting to Manders without tipping him off in advance. By the time I got to the corner he was half into a blue Zodiac. I got in the other side, up front. He was pulling away from the kerb before my reggie reached the upholstery.

"Don't believe in hanging about, do you?"

"I'm supposed to be goin' off home. Them bastards in the office see us pickin' up fares on our own account they get a bit narked. Where's it to?"

"Well now — how's about Buckingham Palace?"

"Visitor are you?"

"All the way from Corn Beef City."

"You don't sound like a Yank."

"It's in Essex." He went into Charing

74

Cross Road and down towards Trafalgar Square. The traffic was pretty heavy. He was about twenty-five, on the thin side. It was a fair bet he wouldn't throw up his mitts in horror at the idea of earning a few bob on the side. "Maybe you and me could do some business, mate," I said.

He gave me a quick look. "We are doin' business, chief, this is a cab, I take people places for money, that's business, innit?"

I felt in my hip pocket and came up with a oncer. "My card," I said, putting it on the window ledge in front of us. He thought about it for a moment, then his left hand did its brown cobra imitation and the quid disappeared.

We shot down past Trafalgar Square. Only the end of April but already people had come thousands of miles to feed our pigeons in our diabolical weather. Don't they have hungry birds in their countries? I'm sure if I went to New York or Paris I'd find better thrills than chucking lentils at their feathered friends.

We went under the big arch into The Mall and I told him to pull in wherever he liked.

We stopped on the St James's Park side. Straight ahead of us down the big avenue was the gold statue in front of the Palace. Some birds were pecking at the grass, hard to say if they were big ducks or small geese.

"I'm a debt-collector," I said when he switched off. "It's worth a couple of quid to me to know a few things about a bloke called Tony Manders, he's a driver at the same place as you."

He frowned, slowly shaking his head. "Sorry, don't know any Manders, no, can't think who you mean, chief."

Two coppers came strolling up from the palace end. A big modern coach with German number plates and tinted windows pulled in about twenty yards ahead of us. Two old American ladies stopped the coppers for a map-reading session. Out of the coach piled a mob of krauts with cameras, most of the men wearing those green felt overcoats, like horse-blankets with pleats down the back. Their guide issued an ultimatum and they went quick marchen to der Queen's haus.

We both saw these things without

really looking at them. We were in a different city.

I brought out another note. Come to think of it he did know Manders.

"All I want to know is when he starts work — I've a few points to put to him and I hear he's the sort to go ducking and diving if he smells bother. I'd also like to have his home address. Without him knowing of course."

"You goin' to hurt him, are you?"

"No, course not!" He snorted cynically. I smiled. We both kept looking straight ahead. "I'm not, as it happens — worry you if I was, would it?"

"I don't give a monkey's, chief. He ain't my best friend — he's one of them who wants to ship all us coons back home, innee? That's okay by me, I told him, you and Enoch give me two grand I'll go back home like a shot — I was born in Herne Hill, wasn't I? London south-east twenty-eight! You'll have to do better than two quid though."

"You tell me what car he's got and when he's due in the office and I'll give you four. I'll give you the same again if you finger him for me. And the address, of course."

I showed him the next two quid. He nodded and it changed ownership.

Brown fingers, white fingers, green money.

"He's got a blue Cortina. He'll report in there about nine tonight, he always works at night, gets more out of punters goin' home pissed from the West End. He'll sign in the book and wait till they give him a fare. After that he'll get his jobs from the radio."

"Very good. I'll wait on the corner of Gerrard Street, half-eight. You bring the address and hang about till he shows and I bung you the four, okay? I give you my sacred word, he won't get hurt any more than is necessary."

"Be a hard geezer to hurt, chief, he's had a coupla dust-ups I know of, goes a bit berserk."

"His mum didn't have inner harmony I expect. What's your name by the way? Mine's Jim."

"Everton."

"Okay, Everton, if you go back by Piccadilly you can drop me around Half Moon Street."

We drove past the big gates of the Palace. People had come halfway round the world to stick their heads between the railings to see a couple of toy soldiers playing bootsie in front of a sentry-box.

* * *

Back in the office I phoned a bloke I knew in the music game, Reg Moorcock, an optimist who used to live near us in Dagenham. I sometimes bumped into him in the West End. He had this ambition to write songs for Sinatra or Max Bygraves but so far he hadn't even made the Eurovision Song heats. We weren't old mates exactly but it's always nice to meet a face you can put a past to.

After the usual ration of long time no see and how's yer father I asked if he'd ever come across a bloke called Philip Beevers.

"He's got a partner in your line — Lou Nicholas is it?"

"Oh *him*! Lou Nicholas pon my life. Mr Slippery in person. I know who you mean now. They had an open-air festival up Lincoln way last summer — the usual story, ten thousand stinkin' hippies in tents chantin' and freakin' out, all that guru cobblers. Yeah, one toilet in a three-mile radius and mass indignation among the yokels about drugs and litter. And Oh Dear where did the gate money go when the groups wanted payin'."

"I read about that one. He had it away with the take, did he?"

"They said it was a dead loss cos the punters slipped in without payin' — they always do, don't they? Lou Nicholas, Jewish-like but the public school sort, smooth as a bun penny, stare at you with his big blue minces and tell you the most diabolical lyin' crap you ever did hear. Don't do no business with him, Jim me old son."

"It's Beevers I'm dealing with. Seems to be loaded."

"He won't be for long if he's partners with Lou bleeding Nicholas. I have heard it said there's a firm of villains could be tied up with him, don't know if that's for true or not."

"A proper firm? What sort of line are they in?"

"Couldn't tell you."

"Yeah well, I'm much obliged to you, Reg. Doing any good in the song-writing game are you? Any big hits coming up?"

"Only the wife."

Next I rang Beevers at the office number he'd given me in the Aldwych. The girl said Topaz Artiste Management and then asked me to hang on because Mr Beevers was taking a call from Amsterdam. I had to wait a couple of minutes.

"Jim Hazell, Mr Beevers — thought I'd let you know I've tracked Manders down. I'm hoping to see him tonight. I've been to the undertakers, the girl thought it sounded like a bloke about his age. You want me to give a buzz after I've seen him?"

"Suppose he denies it flat — you've got no direct evidence?"

"I'll play it by ear. Meantime I think I'll nip up and see Thornton."

"Go easy on him, Jim — if it is him, which I doubt, well, he probably just went a bit bonkers. I wouldn't want to be vindictive."

"Okay — one thing, better get your locks changed, eh?"

"I've already put wheels in motion on that. Tell you what — we won't be at home tonight, we're at a private dinner in the Hilton — why don't you come along afterwards and have a drink? Just ask at the desk — I'm with Mr Thomas's party."

"I'll see how I'm placed."

"We'll be breaking up about eleven. By the way, I should be careful with Manders."

"So should I by the sound of him. Oh yeah — how old's your wife, Mr Beevers?"

"Twenty-six — why?"

"He guessed wrong then — the joker I mean, he told the undertaker girl she was twenty-eight."

I thought we'd been cut off. Then he spoke. "You're sure about that — he said twenty-*eight*?"

"Yeah, I made a point of it, thought it could give us a clue how well he knows you both."

"She is twenty-six."

★ ★ ★

I locked up and went downstairs. Christine had a couple of her secretarial girls in there picking up their greens. I sat quietly till they clomped off in their platform boots.

"Hark to them, moving with all the elegance of Guards recruits — don't girls want to look like girls any more?"

"Men are doing it for them." She was in a black dress with white lace cuffs and neck. Under the desk her legs looked terrific, on the small side but the way women's legs used to look. "Oh dear," I said, "I was going to take you out to a new restaurant tonight only I'm landed with this bleeding job, you'd have liked it, the new chef's all the way from Aldershot, nothing wrong with army cooks — "

"I'm going out to dinner with my cousin from Sussex."

"That's all right then. Oh well, keep moving's the motto. Have a nice time with your cousin."

"Au revoir." She could be quite brisk at times. I felt a bit disappointed. I

83

don't know what it is with me and women, when I'm feeling low I call it loneliness and when I'm flourishing I call it freedom.

Still, I was doing all right these days. If you can call it flourishing when your Friday night date is a psychopathic minicab cowboy who likes punching women.

5

THERE was a bit of red in the sky when I turned off Highbury Park and down Avenell Road past the big red stands of the Arsenal football ground. Been there a few times as a kid, hanging about the entrance to see the stars come out after a Saturday game.

The lights were on inside the main entrance but after all these years I still couldn't see the marble halls they're always mentioning in the papers.

Couldn't see any of today's big stars either, all at home in their ranch-style mansions in Hertfordshire I expect.

Gillespie Road is like any other street near the big football grounds, little terraced houses in the shadows of the monster stadium, barbed wire on the back walls to stop the soccer hordes from dropping in for tea.

I could see the London Transport sign as I got out of the car. How many times had I come through that tube station with my mates? Up the long dark tunnel from the platforms, the one with a separate mesh-wired rabbit run so that any non-sporting punter doesn't have to fight upstream against the football Niagara . . . out into the daylight, the big rush to the turnstiles, the geezers flogging popcorn and hamburgers and early papers and rosettes and badges . . .

I just don't believe I'm thirty-four. Where did it all go?

It was only five o'clock, not many about. I found the number and opened the little gate and crossed the front garden in four steps. Somewhere everybody was watching TV.

She was in her fifties, biggish, grey-haired, round pink face with no lines. She was wearing an electric pink frock and woolly slippers.

"This where Mr Thornton lives, luv?" I said with a nice smile to prove I wasn't The Strangler.

"I'm afraid Mr Thornton has passed away," she said calmly. "I'm his wife — what was it about?"

"Passed away? I'm ever so sorry to hear that. Was it recent?"

"A week last Tuesday. Are you from the insurance?"

"No, I'm from Mr Beevers as it happens."

"Oh." She stepped back and held the door open. "You'd better come in, I've been expecting it."

A younger woman appeared at the end of the lobby. "What is it, Mum?" She was the smart sort, chunky shoes and a blue coat with brass buttons, dark hair done up in a high bouffant. Mrs Thornton closed the door. The house had a waxy smell but not unpleasant. The daughter eyed me as hospitably as if I'd brought the eviction notice.

In the front sitting-room Mrs Thornton switched off the telly. It was a small room like ten million others, too much furniture, hand-coloured photos of kids next to a black-and white wartime wedding-group on the mantelpiece, a sofa facing the fire, all the light coming from the bowl in the middle of the ceiling, a *TV Times* on a sagging easy chair, the telly at an angle to the tiled fireplace, the smooth red glow of smokeless coal in the grate, a curly rug in front of the hearth, a budgie in a cage by the window.

I'd been brought up in that room, though not that actual version of it, if you follow.

Mrs Thornton picked the *TV Times* off the chair saying apologetically, "We always meant to have it re-covered." She had one of those round, smooth country faces that go on looking young for ever. Under her thick brown stockings her right leg was heavily bandaged from ankle to knee. It felt exactly like I was a stranger calling on my own Mum.

The daughter kept clocking me with hard eyes.

"My name's James Hazell," I said. "I didn't have any idea your husband was dead, Mrs Thornton, I'm very sorry about barging in like this — "

"What is it exactly you want?" the daughter demanded.

"I'm working for Mr Beevers. He's been having a spot of bother lately and there was just a chance Mr Thornton could've helped — was he ill for long, Mrs Thornton?"

"Depends what you mean by ill. He

took his own life." Her voice was calm and quiet.

"Could I ask what you mean when you said you'd been expecting it?"

She sat down on the sofa and folded her hands on her lap. They'd seen more hard work than soft soothing oils. "He didn't tell me anything about it until — "

The daughter stepped sharply between us. "Don't say anything, Mum — "

"It's time you were home, June, Wally will be wanting his tea."

"Wally can wait. I'm not leaving you here alone — "

"June was very upset with her Dad going like that," Mrs Thornton said to me.

"Yes, must've been a shock for you," I said, looking at Mrs Thornton round June's hips. She had very good legs. I was ashamed of myself for noticing.

"Yes, it was a terrible shock," June snapped, "the *terrible* part was Moneybags Beevers giving my Dad the sack for no good reason — I should hope he is having bother, I hope he's having a whole lot of bother, it makes me bloody sick to think of ponces like that spending more in a

89

night than most people have to bring up their families, that's what's *terrible* Mr whatever your name is — "

"We know why your Dad got the sack, June," the mother said patiently, "he started taking a drop when he was working and you can't have that, not when you're a showfure."

"It was working for that Beevers started him on the bottle, he never done any drinking in his other jobs, did he? Then he sacks him — just like that, after four years? And now he's sending the heavy mob round because he's having a spot of bother? I know the bother I'd like to give him."

"I'm only making a few inquiries," I said. "Beevers has been having practical jokes played on him, then yesterday somebody got into his flat and sprayed black paint over his wife's clothes. Whoever done it had a key so naturally he's assumed it has to be somebody who's been close to him — he also knew when Mrs Beevers had her weekly hairdo. All I'm doing is having a word with everybody who's worked for him. I'm sure — "

"He went into their flat and put paint all over her clothes?" Mrs Thonton said, shaking her head. "All Bert ever done was — "

"Don't say anything, Mum!"

"All he did was what?" I said.

Before the daughter could stop her Mrs Thornton said, "Bert cut things out of the papers and sent them in for Mr Beevers. He told me the day before he . . . "

"Do shut up, Mum!"

"I think you'd better be off home, June." When these mild people finally cut loose the change can be a bit frightening. She more or less pushed June out of the room. I heard them at it in the lobby then the sound of June's hard shoes on the pavement. Mrs Thornton came back into the little warm sitting-room.

"I'm sorry about that, Mr Hazell, June thinks she's protecting me — "

"Mrs Thornton, can I get it straight — your husband cut coupons out of the papers and sent them off in Beevers's name? Insurance and things like that?"

"He told me on the Monday night. I wouldn't like you to know the state he was in, weeping and — next day, Tuesday, I came back from doing my shopping and he'd done it. Gas. Took his own life while the balance of his mind was disturbed, that's what they said at the inquest. Poor old Bert."

We sat in silence, looking at the fire. Smokeless fuel doesn't have proper flames either. Nothing's the same, is it?

"Mrs Thornton — your husband say anything about phone calls?"

She began to shake her head.

"I'm sure Bert would've mentioned it, he was so ashamed of himself, sending off all those things he'd cut out, he said he wanted me to understand, he wasn't himself these last two or three months. He went a bit strange, the doctor said it was severe depression. Course he was always a bit quiet, Bert, you know, made you think there was deep things going on inside."

"Did he leave you any money?"

She looked at the fire and then at me. "We had a few hundred in the building society."

"Beevers told me he gave him five grand, you know, five thousand."

"Oh — you know about that?" She made a little grimace. "Bert told me about it that Monday. He said it hadn't been done official, I was to keep it hidden and use it in emergencies — I'm so worried, I don't know what to do with it. All that money in the house. I haven't even told June and Wally."

"Hang on to it, luv. Beevers isn't putting it through his books so the tax need never hear about it. You could bung a fiver into the Post Office every week, as if you was saving it. Got a loose floorboard anywhere you could stow it under for safety?"

"There's a part of the floor in the kitchenette."

"You put it in a tin box to keep the damp out and shove it in there. Don't worry, thousands of villains are getting away with it so why not you, eh?"

She looked at me for a moment and then felt a flap pocket on her frock. "I haven't told anybody about this, either." She brought out a blue envelope folded in two. "Not even June's seen this."

There was nothing on the envelope. I straightened it out and pulled out a sheet of blue writing-paper. The writing was small with a back slope.

Dear Ida,

This is the best way. I can't go on putting you through all the worry of looking after me. If Mr Beevers finds out it was me sent those things tell him I was not in my proper mind. It wasn't his fault, tell him, I should've taken the responsibility like a man. He'll understand. You've given me a wonderful life, Ida, please try to keep only the good memories of me. Tell June I always loved her and little Gary, it was my not being well that caused the rows.

Good-bye sweetheart, till we'll meet again.

Your loving husband,
Bert.

She watched me read it. I had a job to keep my face together. I put the sheet back in the envelope and handed it back. "Do you know what he meant?" she asked. I felt for my fags and then decided she had a right to know why her husband had gone to pieces.

"Your husband had an accident, he couldn't help it, bloke stepped out in front of Beevers's car in Leicester Square, it was raining and dark — the bloke was killed. Your husband wanted to go straight to the police but Beevers said nobody saw it and made him drive on. Hit and run, obviously worried him sick."

Her shoulders fell. "Poor Bert," she said softly, looking into the red glow, "why didn't he tell me?"

"Felt too guilty I expect. Beevers said he had to give him the sack because he could've got involved in more accidents — drinking and that."

She shook her head slowly. "At first Bert said he was glad to be finished with that job, he said Mr Beevers was getting mixed up in other things. Course he didn't realize till later it wasn't going to be easy getting another job at his age. He got so depressed he wouldn't even leave the house in the end. Poor Bert."

"You know what sort of things he meant Beevers was mixed up in?"

"No, he never actually said. He kept

mentioning a partner — would Nicholas be his name?"

"Would he have told you if he'd been making hoax phone calls as well as the newspaper adverts?"

"I think he would have — he said he wanted to tell me everything. Poor Bert."

"One thing's for sure, he didn't do this latest paint job. Anyway, I'd better not bother you any more, Mrs Thornton — tell you what, I'll give you my office number, you give me a ring if there's anything I can help you about. I mean it, just give me a shout."

"It's very good of you."

"And bung that money under the floor and use it as you need it and don't tell a blooming soul about it. All right?"

I wrote the number on a sheet of the same blue writing-paper as her husband's note and she saw me to the door.

"You'll be a regular on the North Bank I expect," I said, nodding in the direction of the stadium behind the houses. She laughed.

"I've never been inside that place

96

once," she said. "Course I've spoken to some of them — that Mr Mercer? He's a manager now, I see him on the television, I used to speak to him in the street when he was a player here, ever such a nice man he were."

I was just going to say good-bye when we both heard the footsteps.

Soon as I saw him I knew he had to be June's husband. June wasn't two yards behind.

"What's all this about then?" he demanded. He was a solid bloke about forty, going bald, open shirt, brown cardigan.

"For goodness sake calm yourself, Wally," said Mrs Thornton.

"I wanna know what's going on here," he demanded, blocking the path.

Half the street must have heard him. He was definitely ready to stick one on me. Anything I did was going to be wrong.

Mrs Thornton went right up against him. "Don't you dare speak to a visitor of mine like that, Wally, what Mr Hazell and me was discussing is none of your concern."

I was unlocking the Stag when he came charging up the pavement. "I don't want any more of your fakking crap, I wanna know why you was pestering the old lady," he announced.

Over his shoulder I saw June and Mrs Thornton arguing at the gate. It was a very delicate situation.

With as much of a smile as I could drag up I tapped his chest with my middle finger. "I wouldn't want to upset Mrs Thornton so let's you and me get in the motor and have a quiet chat, eh? Only don't get stroppy with me — all right?"

I gave his shoulder a friendly pat. He'd been around long enough to know what a heavy sounds like. It's the friendliness of it all that shakes you rigid. Sir Oliver himself couldn't have acted the part better. He retreated. I gave Mrs Thornton a wave and drove off.

Back up Avenell Road the lights were still on inside the Arsenal entrance. Funny, you go to a place like Highbury Stadium over thirty years and you always see the same little houses and the same bit of broken pavement but it isn't *your* bit of pavement, a million other people know it just as well and they've never heard of *you*.

That's what it is about London, millions of us passing through and hardly leaving any mark at all.

On the other hand — that's what makes us a bit different, isn't it? Your Londoner's got to make his own luck because if he lies down to die there's not a lot will stop to ask what's wrong.

You've given me a wonderful life, Ida.

Would I ever have somebody I could write to like that?

★ ★ ★

The West End on a Friday night. All the glamour of a honeymoon in a gravelpit. Places that charge double and a million people trying to get a kick out of looking at a million people. Plus the freaks and weirdos, nutters of every description, all bombing about Leicester Square and Piccadilly Circus and Soho looking for something to screw or something to steal or something to smash to bits.

Nobody knows anybody in the West End, you can get the maniac out of your system and then go home and play normal till your next attack. Some of them are only mutterers, some of them shout their heads off at nobody in particular. Then there's the occasional nutter with a blade in his pocket for the first unlucky punter who bumps into him accidentally.

One time when I was about twelve I came up West with a bunch of my mates — we were living in south Hackney then. Going down Shaftesbury Avenue this big spade in a silk suit and pure white shirt comes out of a posh restaurant with a blonde in tow.

She's in a shiny white gown, all the way to the pavement. She was *lovely*. The spade snaps his fingers and a cab stops immediately, just like the movies. They shoot off among all the glamorous electric adverts and we stand there saying the disgusting things you'd expect from a bunch of twelve-year-old patriots.

All the time we're thinking — cor, give us some of that!

The West End was dead swanky in those days. You had the feeling the rozzers would nab you for not wearing a clean shirt and tie.

Nowadays? The cops can hardly get on their helmets for their hairstyles.

Never mind Memory Lane, dumbo — what about this job?

A chilly Friday night on the corner of Chinese Gerrard Street with your guts churning on two alleged hamburgers isn't ideal conditions for deep thoughts, you'll find, should you be so lucky.

I couldn't see any sense to it. Thornton did the coupons to pay Beevers back for the hit and run but he didn't do the other things, not unless graveyards aren't as strict as they used to be.

Two jokers?

If that was it Beevers was in worse trouble than he knew. He had to be holding back about his private affairs. Still, he was paying me good money to stop this malarkey, not expose his darkest secrets.

Nobody pays you for investigating the client!

At twenty to nine Everton, the Herne

101

Hill immigrant, came sliding down the twilight street like a shadow with a bad conscience. He walked past me into Gerrard Street. I caught up with him and he slowed down. About half the people strolling past us were Chinese.

You could tell them apart easy enough, they were the ones who looked at home.

"I got the address," he said, "you got the bread?"

We swopped bits of paper. The address was in Tierney Road, Streatham Hill. We took up position opposite the minicab entrance, under the awning of a Chinese restaurant. On the other side of the glass this loving couple were leaning over the table to whisper soft noodles at each other. It was a lot colder on our side of the glass.

Everton watched the traffic over my shoulder. It was a long ten minutes. We didn't have much to talk about, both of us born Londoners but only half an accent in common.

Then the blue Cortina came sliding down from Shaftesbury Avenue. "That's him," said Everton. The Cortina found a parking space about fifteen yards farther down on the other side.

Everton took off into the night. I was across the road and doing my semi-pissed act in the narrow doorway by the time Manders turned into the entrance.

6

YOU wonder witnesses are always picking the wrong bloke at police line-ups? Not one of the people I'd spoken to had told me the obvious fact about Tony Manders. He was big and he had a rocker's greasy hairstyle and he dressed the part, brown leather jerkin, flower shirt open to the belly, fawn flareds with a broad belt and big buckle, square-toed shoes with red and blue uppers.

Only he had a girl's face.

Soft red cheeks with no trace of shadow or stubble. No lines under his eyes. No spots, bruises or scratches.

His forehead was small and narrow and his thinnish nose was higher up on his face than is usual with men.

On top of all that he had a rosebud mouth and light green eyes, long dark lashes, thin eyebrows.

With a boat-race like that he must have been belting other blokes all his life just to prove he was normal.

"This where I get a cab, mate?" I said, blinking and looking ten pints gone.

"You're in luck, squire," he said, "big queue upstairs, my cab's outside."

He steered me to the Cortina. I got in the back. He got in and twisted round. He was smiling. "Bin having a few drinks, yeah?" he said. "Where's it to be then?"

I blinked stupidly. I said the first thing that came into my noddle. "Ehm — uhm — just off Stockwell Road — I got this bird to see only I forget the actual address, I'll know it when I see it."

"I'll find it for you, squire, lucky you bumped into me there, up the office they'd have most likely shoved you on to one of the coons, most of them berks can't hardly speak the language let alone take you anywhere. Make any sense to you, filling up the country with them fakking nig-nogs when we ain't got enough jobs or houses for our own?"

He came out left into Shaftesbury Avenue and down to Piccadilly Circus. It was getting dark.

Driving was a duel to the death the

way he went at it. Round into Haymarket he even managed to give a bus a fright and that isn't common.

"Bus drivers, think they own the fakking roads," he said, sitting back at his ease, driving with one hand only. "I got no time for them bastards," he said, "you see all this violence against the conductors and that? Know what it really is? It's the public fighting back, squire, that's all it is."

"Yeah?"

We went round Trafalgar Square. The floodlights were on the fountains and the white buildings. He had one solution to every problem — shove the pedal down.

"Tell you another thing, squire, in this job you see a helluva lot of bad driving, right? Know what I can do? I can tell you from the way a motor's driven what kind of driver it's got. I ain't boasting. I don't have to. There's foreigners — French and Eyties and that. Then there's women and coons. You see something really stoopid you'll find nine times outa ten it's a bird or a nig-nog. Women — they can never make up their bleeding minds what to do. Nig-nogs — they make up their minds but it's always to do something diabolical. Not their fault I suppose, they just ain't got the brains for it. Enoch Powell, squire, he knows the score."

He terrorized a couple of family-type saloons on the race down into Whitehall. I was beginning to see where the James Bond films made the money. Daggers on the wheels and machine-guns up the exhaust would've been this lunatic's idea of happy motoring. We went past the Cenotaph at such a lick I had to look out the back window to make sure it hadn't been shifted.

All the time I was trying to think up some subtle manoeuvre.

We shot across Parliament Square and along the side of the House of Commons to the Embankment. He was still rabbiting on about making Britain white man's territory once again.

The hell with it, when in doubt have it out.

First off I lobbed in a tester.

"Friend of mine's having some bother with an anonymous hoaxer," I said. "Bastard ordered two minicabs for him the other night, both turned up at once. Embarrassing for him, wasn't it? You get a lot of that funny stuff in your job?"

He delved into the glove-compartment and found some chewing-gum. "Yeah, lot of clever fakkers about," he said. "The legit cabbies used to do a lotta that to mess the minicabs about."

"This friend of mine thinks it could be a driver he had working for him." He said nothing. Lambeth Bridge went by and he stepped on it for the straight run along the Embankment. "Anyway, next thing this nutter breaks into my friend's flat and slaughters a load of clothes with paint."

The lights stopped us at Vauxhall Bridge. He tapped the wheel with his fingertips. "You've sobered up a bit quick, chief."

"Me? I haven't had a drop all day."

We sailed across the big wide bridge. A block of flats on the south side was using more electricity than two small towns. Some film star lives there, I remember reading, must have a terrific view of the river. I thought I saw little figures moving behind the big windows, your show biz suavos having an exclusive dinner-party, I expect, witty gossip and plenty of After Eight mints. Manders wasn't saying a lot.

When in doubt have it out.

"My friend's name is Beevers."

Silence. We stopped at the red coming off the bridge. "Thought there has to be something dodgy about you," he said, "one of Lou Nicholas's team are you? How'd you find me? That's it — Adriana, you went up there looking for me and — "

"I don't know any Adriana."

"That crazy little cow's the only way you could've found me. I'll bloody well — so, Beevers thinks I've been playing naughty tricks on him, does he?"

"Have you?"

"I'm going to tell you, am I?"

We came off Vauxhall Bridge and then under the bridge that carries the overground railway lines from Waterloo. He pulled into the side at a bit of old pavement the road engineers forgot to roll up and take away. He put on the inside light and twisted round. He gave me a grin. He didn't look so pretty when you saw the big red hands and the nails chewed down to vanishing point. We were stopped in the middle of nowhere, a high dark wall on one side, a stink of petrol, the slithery squeaking of tyre-treads from the traffic racing by on the other side.

"So what you aim to do then, mate?"

"Find out if you're the one and tell you to pick another hobby if you are."

The pretty girl's eyes tried to stare me down. "And if I admit it you turn me in — or what?"

"No, he don't want any fuss with the law."

"I'll bet he don't."

"What does that mean?"

"Don't be stoopid, I know the score. If he's getting aggro it's got to do with that Lou Nicholas creep." He was still smiling but his voice changed dramatically, "Now piss off, *Shirley*, before I lose my temper with you."

It's the fair curls. I keep them as short as possible but apart from getting hot tongs from a West Indian barber I can't see any cure for them. Luckily I was too mature to be thumping people every time

110

I got a bit needled. Not a lot of money in it for a start.

"I'll piss off when I'm ready, sonny," I said. "You telling me you don't know about these little capers?"

"That's it in a nutshell, *Shirley*. If I want to chivvy that fat ponce Beevers I won't be playing any kids' games with him, tell him that. And tell him not to bother sending any more wankers like you snooping round behind my back, okay? Now, give me the ninety pee and then get outa the cab — *Shirley*."

I opened the door. "See you in the small claims court."

I got out on the narrow bit of pavement under the big dark wall. The cosy weekend crowd went slithering by in the rush to escape from the nasty, dirty city.

"Just a minute, *Shirley*," said Manders, coming up out of the nearside door.

I'd been reckoning on it but I was dumb enough to expect some more of the old verbals beforehand.

He whacked me without any warning at all, right on the throat. I put my hands back to stop myself falling. I was an easy target for the next one, bang into my guts.

My insides started stampeding up my throat. I tried to turn my face away. He whacked me somewhere about the right eye.

I fell back against the car, making funny choking noises. My tongue was jamming my throat and my stomach was fighting to have a look at all this daylight it kept hearing about.

He caught me by the sweater neck and next bloody thing he was waving a shiny blade in front of my valuable face.

"You mustn't try to dodge paying, *Shirley*."

I got my lungs going again. Our faces were very close. He didn't seem pretty in the slightest. His breath wasn't so clever either. He kept the blade in front of my face but he let go of my sweater to reach inside my jacket pockets.

"And tell Nicholas if he's using amateurs he'll have to send you mob-handed next time — *Shirley*."

I smacked the knife hand away with my left forearm and smacked my forehead into his nice, thin, girlish hooter.

I gave him the heel of my left hand in the eye and jumped sideways and had a kick at his knife hand.

In the dark, under the big bridge, cars racing past to jolly weekends in executive-style estates, that's where it all happened between Tony Manders and me, just a couple of average Londoners who'd got off on the wrong foot.

I belted him again and the knife dropped, bringing it all down to a sporting contest. Heads, boots, knees — he was a difficult bloke to say good-bye to.

When he tried to get the knife off the floor I gave him a volley in the ribs. That's one thing bargain shoes are good for.

Even then I was putting on the brakes. That's something they never tell you about fighting, how *intimate* it is. I mean, you'd never get that close to a bloke if you liked him.

Well, *you* might, Julian.

Enjoying it, that was the red light.

He got up slowly. "Let's have a chat — " I began to say. He came at me in a crouch.

I got my hands on the back of his head and shoved his face down on my raised knee. He collapsed slowly, like a chocolate soldier in a frying pan. I got down on my haunches and pulled his face round by the hair.

"What's all this about Nicholas and his team?"

He groaned. I opened the nearside door to let the passenger light get at him. We were hidden from the traffic, if it mattered. You see many Friday night suburbanites stopping under a dark bridge to ask why two blokes are kicking shit out of each other?

He didn't look too pretty by then. His eyes were closed and his lips were swelling out something horrible. His nose was spluttering blood bubbles. Maybe I'd done him a favour.

I left him and picked up the knife by the blade, sliding it carefully into my jacket pocket. I knelt beside him again.

"You all right?"

More sick noises. I got hold of his hair again, giving it a twist. "So what was you saying? Lou Nicholas — what kind of villainy is he at? Don't do the

114

moody on me again or I'll accommodate you properly next time."

"I don't know nothing," he groaned. I tightened my grip on his greasy hair. He twisted his head in pain. "He's got minders for his shops, that's all I know — leggo, you're pulling it out! I heard him telling Beevers they was necessary to keep the shops in order — that's all I know, straight up."

"What kind of shops?"

"I dunno."

"Was you and Mrs Beevers at it?"

"Nah, she shows out but it's only to see if you'll try your hand, then she says she'll tell him."

I loosened my grip. He was dead still for a moment, waiting to see if I had worse in mind. "She having it off with anybody you know of?" I said.

"Oh yeah, she tells me all her secrets, don't she? I heard him and her having a ruck about Nicholas, that's all."

"What kind of row?"

"He said she was giving Nicholas encouragement, that's all I heard."

"And you got no idea at all what Nicholas is into?"

He shook his head. He was sniffing and gulping like a small boy. I stood up. "All right then," I said, "just remember I know where to find you plus I got a weapon with your dabs on it — you won't be doing anything silly, will you?"

He came up stiffly, shaking his head. I let him get in the car. He wiped his face with a Kleenex from under the dash-board and then started her up. I waited till his red lights were round the corner then I took the knife out of my pocket, holding it by the blade, and placed it close against the foot of the wall.

Nobody would spot it there easily and the rain couldn't get at it to wash off his prints.

I had it across the road on my toes and caught a cab back over Vauxhall Bridge. When I switched on the passenger light there was a small rip on my right knee and my hands were dirty. The rest of the damage added up to aches and bruises, some tender parts round my cheekbones, a lump in my throat and the taste of blood when I licked my lips.

The lengths some people will go to dodge a taxi fare!

* * *

I remembered the Sillitoe girl as I was heading for Christine's flat in the Edgware Road. It was still only a quarter to ten. I tried to phone her from the Post Office boxes in Seymour Street behind Marble Arch but she wasn't in the book and directory had nothing for Sillitoe or Manders.

I got back in the motor and cursed my luck for a Mum who brought me up to keep promises.

By the time I got to Adelaide Road for the second time I was doing over fifty and jumping reds. I pressed her button a few times before anything happened.

Being Friday night groups of young things were skipping past with bottles of wine, the girls in the gear Gran used to wear, the blokes with long hair and strap-bags and the spring-heeled way of walking you get with sandshoes.

Don't knock it, I told myself, that's real life they're enjoying, not hanging about on doorsteps and kicking total strangers under railway bridges.

A window opened up above. I had to step back. "Who is it?" she was calling down.

"Jim Hazell, I got to see you, I had a — "

"I'm in bed, go away, you'll waken Duffy."

"Manders might be up here — "

Her head went in and another head came out, hair about the same length. "You deaf?" a man's voiced snarled. "Piss off or I'll come down and do you."

"Look, I'm only — "

Her head came out beside his. "Go away or I'll call the police."

I groaned and closed my eyes. Then I saw the funny side to it. My ribs ached when I laughed.

"Manders is coming," I shouted, "better get your trousers on, squire."

As I limped down the steps I heard that same typewriter still clacking away. Maybe he was writing one of these searching novels about Man's eternal questing and that. Pity he didn't have time to look out the window.

★ ★ ★

It was half past ten.

I headed for Christine's flat. Soothing, that's what I needed, a hot bath and soft hands.

7

I LET myself into Christine's flat and turned on the hall light. All my bruises were aching. I went to the bathroom and got the hot tap running. Then I went to the bedroom.

As I opened the door I heard these grunting noises. I switched on the light. The blankets were jumping about.

"You're not doing that on your own, are you?" I asked.

The shapes under the blankets went still. Her head appeared slowly. She stared at me, her hands holding the sheet across her mouth.

"You look just like Kilroy who was here," I said.

She blinked a lot. "I didn't think you would be coming."

"Interrupt your dinner, did I?"

The other shape moved and a head of fair hair came to the surface. Nice-looking kid, about twenty, well fed. He seemed a bit scared.

"This is my cousin Bobby," she said.

"Wotcha, Bobby — no, don't move, I'll just get a clean shirt and be on my way."

She got out of bed and put on a dressing-gown. I opened the wardrobe and lifted the dark blue shirt off its hanger, plus my yellow tie.

"For God's sake, Jim, say *something*!"

I turned my head. "Rain seems to be holding off."

"Look — Bobby and I went to dinner, we had a bottle of wine — "

"Very nice, too. Think this tear in my trousers will show? I'm nipping down to the Hilton for a few drinks."

"It was my fault, actually," he said. Very educated accent. I gave him a smile.

"Sorry about bursting in, old man, I'll just have a quick sluice down and then I won't bother you people again." She looked exasperated.

"I wish you'd stop acting blasé, it's most embarrassing, you — "

I stopped in the doorway. "That's what's wrong with your generation, Titch, you've been brainwashed with these outdated conventions. Take yer fun where you find it I always say."

When I came out of the bathroom she was waiting in the hall. She looked really upset. I examined my tie in the mirror.

"You think I'm *low*, don't you?" she said in her little girl's voice.

"On the short side maybe. See you later then."

"God, I hate you when you're trying to be superior — "

I patted the top of her head. "Don't worry so, Titch, there's people out there doing ten times worse."

Tell the truth I was disappointed. Always the same, you only realize how much she means when you see her with another bloke.

★ ★ ★

The Hilton foyer was full of Americans and Japanese telling each other how many more museums they had to look forward to. It took the desk about ten minutes to locate Beevers at the private dinner party. The hard currency crowd charged up and down. All these grey-haired Yanks and clockwork Japs probably once met face to face in the Pacific I was thinking. I didn't see any back-slapping reunions.

When Beevers saw me he frowned.

"What happened? Better tell me about it in the washroom."

Standing in front of the mirror I had another butcher's at my face. It didn't look too bad. At the other end of the basins three small Japanese geezers in identical dark suits and spiky black haircuts were rabbiting away to each other. Strange sort of lingo, can't ever see it catching on here. Beevers was in a midnight blue suit with a lighter blue shirt and dark blue tie. His eyes had that moist look, booze or emotion was hard to tell.

"I've solved part of the mystery and I also had a run-in with Tony Manders," I said.

"You had a fight with him?"

"Just breaking the ice by his standards. Point is, Mr Beevers, Thornton sent off all them adverts in your name, only — "

"Bert Thornton? I don't believe it! He actually admitted it, did he?"

"Not to me, to his missus. He's dead.

123

Those gents up there have a word for it, cash and carry, hari-kari. Gassed himself, last Tuesday. Severe depression the doctor said. He didn't get another job."

He looked round quickly but the three Japs thought our lingo was pretty inscrutable, too. He was astounded and shocked and eaten up with regret and that. I kept thinking he was a right shit but on the other hand he had given the bloke five grand, which was something. A quid for washing the car, five grand for busting up a life.

"Anyway, Mr Beevers, he couldn't have done the paint caper. And he couldn't have phoned the undertakers. So you got two jokers on your hands."

His mouth was hanging open. His railings were not too clever, too much brown among the gold. Two Yanks came into the washroom saying wasn't this guy Williamson one of the great Macbeths? At least with them you know the words.

"What about Manders?"

I shrugged. "I don't think he's had anything to do with it. Fact I'm sure of it. He seemed to think I was a

124

heavy working for your partner. That mean anything to you?"

He frowned. The two Yanks came past on their way out, this time telling each other wasn't the grass rilly green?

"You sure Manders couldn't have been lying?" he said, "I mean, he was bound to deny it, I — "

"I'd bet on it, Mr Beevers. By the way, any chance of a drink? I'm as dry as a lizard's tit."

"Yes, come on, we'll have a quick one and then go back to my place."

"How much do you want your wife to know?"

He stopped in his tracks. The three Japs had to come between us to get to the door. We stared at each other over their jet black spikes.

"What about my wife?" he demanded.

"You might be better to hear it first — no point in putting any more scares into her, is there?"

"What is there to be scared about?"

"You think it's just everyday stuff, do you, some mystery geezer nipping in and out of your flat and spreading black paint over your clothes? You must lead an exciting life, Mr Beevers."

He dropped his head and let out a big sigh.

"What am I going to do, Jim?"

"If I could have a drink, Mr Beevers — "

We went across the foyer and up to the first floor, then past the 007 bar. Most of them were middle-aged — it was a dinner to mark the occasion of Mr Thomas being thirty-five years in the music publishing business. Rock and pop had killed off the stuff they knew best but they were all very jolly, plenty in the iron tank and nothing much to worry about except how long it would be before the horrible socialists put a tax on sunshine.

Beevers took me across to the bar, a table with a white cloth and a bottle of everything. I could see a beer was out of the question so I had a scotch and dry ginger.

Then Mrs Beevers came out of the crowd in tow with a slim Spanish-looking geezer.

No other word for it, she looked sensational. She was in one of those gowns you used to see in films, one arm and shoulder bare, one leg showing when she walked, no back to it until your eyes got down to the interesting part. She'd piled her white-gold hair on top with a silver comb at the back. Her neck was long and lovely.

Something else — she smiled when she saw me!

She kept smiling at me while Beevers introduced me to Lou Nicholas. He was that dark, shiny type, too smooth to put a firm date on, maybe thirty, maybe more.

"Jim's been giving me a few ideas about boosting the furniture side," Beevers said. Nicholas nodded. He'd met more interesting sandwich men.

"You've been in a fight," she said, peering at my various scratches. I shrugged modestly.

"No, I was just watching."

"Must be a risky business, being a peeping tom," Nicholas drawled, with a leer.

"You could be right. I think I'll go back to indecent exposure."

She laughed. Nicholas examined me coldly for a moment then he turned away. Standing that near I saw he wasn't so much thin as well-trained. He had about two hundred quid's worth of mohair on his back, a red shirt with matching hankie, plain black tie, a flat stomach and a narrow waist. His black hair was parted near the middle and combed straight back the old-fashioned way. Maybe it was the new fashion. He didn't look the type to miss any important developments.

"I think this lot are about ready to swallow it, let's go home, Simone," Beevers said.

"Go *home*?" she said. She laughed. "You go home if you like, I want to enjoy myself. Lou — what about that new club in Berkeley Square, everybody says it's great fun. You'd like to come with us, wouldn't you, Mr Hazell?"

"Near my bedtime actually — "

"All right, we'll go to the damned place," Beevers said. He gave me a heavy look. "You can stay up late for once, Jim."

A short fat man came round with a menu he was asking everybody to sign. He was Mr Thomas. He kept saying what a wonderful night it had been. His wife came up to make sure he wasn't having another drinkie. She was wearing an off-shoulder creation that must've wowed 'em about the time Joe Louis was Mohammed. She gave Simone a kiss on the cheek and Lou Nicholas a dig in the ribs. I stood back and let them get on with the sincerity while I had another scotch and dry. A man with stooped shoulders and long grey hair bumped into me and said sorry but wasn't it the really important thing in life to have true friends, I mean, we could carve each other up in business but have a laugh about it later because friendship meant more than money, know what I mean, don't you? In this life, when you boil it down, that's all we've got, isn't it, friends, true friends . . .

In the Rolls going to Berkeley Square Beevers said, "Glad that's over, at least in the furniture business we all knew we were bloody enemies."

"That generation had the benefit of a docile public," Nicholas said. "They all seem to be married to the same woman. The one sitting next to me — show biz of the old school, my God, a mouth you could have used to carry the spare wheel. Hard to believe they once had an iron grip on public taste, isn't it?"

He was sitting with Mrs Beevers in the back and I was up front beside Mr Beevers. Life looks a bit different from a Rolls. Even at night people stare through the windows to see who the celebrities are. I expect you could get to like it.

Kirstie's, the new in place, was like all the other in places before it, heavy rock not much louder than the sound of a skyscraper falling on your nut, hooray henries and their model birds rubbing shoulders with the newest pop stars that nobody gets time to hear before their month of stardom is up, drinks at prices that would have paid off the mortgage.

I don't know what the new in dance was called, the fruggle maybe or the crub, the usual group epilepsy anyway.

Money, that was the essential ingredient.

Are you members, sir?

No, but here's a tenner to buy yourself a drink.

You're members, sir.

Champagne? Fifteen quid a bottle?

Give us two for starters.

Mrs Beevers wanted to dance. Mr Beevers nominated Partner Lou for that one. As soon as they were off into the hippy-hippy shake he cupped his hand round his north and south and shoved his face at my left earhole.

"He's a Jewish bastard," he bawled intimately. He drew back to see my face. I just looked at him. "Let's go to the gents and have a talk," he roared. I finished my glass of champers and let him do the pushing to get us out of the in crowd.

"Make a mint these places," he said, looking round the carsi. There were three basins, each with soap. "All right then, Jim, tell me the worst."

"Mr Beevers, I work on the basis that you're paying so you deserve to hear everything I hear. Only it isn't always good news — I've found people often wish I hadn't told them."

"Fire away," he said, swallowing hard and looking about as cheery as the man who overheard his wife ordering the notaste weedkiller.

"First of all, let's cut out all the

bullshit, Mr Beevers — somebody is putting the frighteners on you and your wife. Thornton started it because he went a bit potty and blamed you for not letting him report the hit and run. Then somebody else took over and I'm betting it wasn't Manders. If you want me to nail him I've got to know the score."

"You can't be a hundred per cent sure about Manders. It's possible — "

"But it isn't likely. Come on, Mr Beevers, Thornton told his wife you were mixed up in something. Manders says your partner has a team of minders — you know, like a firm, muscle, soldiers, the heavy troops. He also said something about shops."

"No secret in that, we have a few bookshops — all right, why try to hide it, porn shops. The so-called minders must be the blokes who run the shops, they don't exactly look like off-duty curates. It's all above-board, Jim, soft porn, nothing heavy. Bert Thornton was an old prude — he stopped buying the *Daily Mirror* once it started showing the whole tit."

"Manders also said he heard you and your wife missus having an argument about Lou Nicholas — you said she was encouraging him. That right?"

He stopped looking me in the eye about then. A couple of young toffs came in and sent a magnum or two into the great democracy of the sewers. We pretended to be washing our hands till they went braying back to Honor and Venetia.

"It's true," he said. He caught my eye in the mirror and looked down. "Jim — things aren't — well, I'm fifty-two and she's twenty-eight — you can't blame me for being a bit neurotic when I see younger men making up to her. I told you — I suffer from insecurity." He tried to smile.

"Twenty-eight is she? That's what the anonymous caller told the funeral-parlour girl. You told me she was twenty-six."

"Did I? She lies about her age. As if it bloody matters in your twenties. I keep telling her, wait till you're bloody fifty, then you'll need all the illusions you can get."

"Narrows the field down a bit though

dunnit? Has to be somebody who knows you both pretty well I reckon."

"But what's he doing these things for?"

"You tell me."

"Let's go back into that madhouse. I'll say one thing, Jim, you do a full day's work."

"Yeah, I give up afternoon snooker when I got to be my own boss."

"Exactly! Pity this whole rotten country wasn't self-employed — shake these lazy trade union bastards up a bit. I *never* get a cold or the flu, you know."

"I had the flu last week as it happens. Maybe I haven't been self-employed long enough to be really healthy."

He frowned at me, thinking maybe I was taking the micky.

We went back to the pulsating glamour of London's in crowd. Where's all this energy come from I kept asking myself, watching them all leaping about on the dancing area. If only we could export late-night dancers we'd be tops.

Mrs Beevers put her exquisite mitt on my arm and nodded for me to lend my body for the next struggle.

Why not? There's going to be a thousand years to lay there in the dark telling yourself this modern dancing is a lot of crap.

I didn't even get to hold her. Matter of fact I got closer to six other men than her. She kept smiling at me though.

Back at the table lips did a lot of hard work but nobody heard much above the amplification. Quadrophonic sound I think it's called. It might be the answer to prison. Beevers began to get a bit Brahms and Lizst, if you know what I mean. I noticed Partner Lou giving me the occasional once-over.

I wondered if he'd ask me out to the toilet as well. It was that kind of evening.

★ ★ ★

We came out of there about one o'clock. Beevers got a bit narked when she asked me if I would drive them home in the Rolls as she was tired and he was pissed.

Lou Nicholas said he was going home to Chelsea. He gave her a peck and

135

clapped Beevers on the back and sort of signalled good-bye to me without committing perjury.

Soon as he was round the corner Beevers said, "How come I had to pick a bloody Jewish shark like that smooth bastard for a partner?"

"Shut up, Phil, and give Jim the keys," she said wearily.

"You've got the keys. I hate that bloody man, I really do."

She patted at the pockets of her black fur coat, one of those with tight little curls. She changed her handbag to her left hand and put her right hand into her pocket.

"Oh my God!"

We both looked at her.

Slowly she brought her hand out of the pocket, her face wide with horror.

She had it by the tail. It was a mouse, a white mouse. It was dead. I'd never seen a dead white mouse before but death has a look all of its own.

She held it up for a very long second, staring at it.

Then she threw it down and jumped back and let out a rascal of a scream.

8

WE went over it again and again in the car. They were in the back. Driving the Rolls felt like floating through the streets. Why fight it? This is what it's all about, I thought, plenty of time in the wooden box to tell yourself the rich are shallow and vulgar.

"We had our own cloakroom in the Hilton," she said, "it was at the end of the private banqueting room — nobody could've got in there without somebody seeing — all those old cows with their minks. They'll hardly take their eyes off them."

"You didn't go into your pockets before we reached the nightclub?"

"I can't remember — I couldn't have or I would have felt it."

"If it was there. It could have been put in your pocket at Kirstie's. Only how did the bastard know we'd be at Kirstie's?"

"Followed us," said Beevers. Being

half-pissed he wasn't too sure what was happening.

"What was the ladies' cloakroom like back there?"

"There was a woman there all the time. I even asked her if she was sure my coat would be all right — she said they were meticulous about security."

"Where were the coats?"

"Behind the counter in a part that was set back — you couldn't have reached them without going behind the counter. Oh God, I think I'm going to be sick."

"Want me to stop the car?"

"For God's sake," Beevers mumbled.

"No, I'll be all right," she said. "Who can be doing these horrible things?"

"Did you go into your pockets before you left the flat? He could've bunged it in there on Thursday afternoon."

"It looked fresh dead to me," Beevers said excitedly, as if he'd just solved the *Marie Celeste* mystery.

"What does a dead mouse look like after a day, Mr Beevers? Mrs Beevers — check your pockets again, maybe there's a note."

"No."

"Funny. That crowd at the Hilton, they seemed like decent enough people."

"Don't let it fool you," she said, "they all love each other madly when they've had enough to drink but by Monday morning the knives are out again."

Going along Marylebone Road we passed an accident. A cop in the road was directing the traffic into a single line.

"Look at that man sitting in the gutter," she said, "he's bleeding to death."

"That's why I thought I'd better drive, Mr Beevers," I said, trying to make him feel less insulted. "Worst time of the week for accidents, Friday night, all these piss-artists careering home, joy-riders roaring about in stolen motors, idiots driving up the motorway on the wrong side — you'd have failed the bag test if you'd got involved in any of that."

Grunt. He'd told us twenty times he was a better driver when he'd had a few because he became more careful. They all say that, your company directors and what not. Then in court their brief gives out the usual old crap about my client having been unwise enough to take a glass of wine on top of tablets for nervous exhaustion, working to make Britain great again, m'lud, just because he wrapped his Jaguar round a lamp-post in a pedestrian precint does not necessarily indicate that my client was, in the strictly legal sense of the word, blotto.

When I switched off the engine in the big gloomy basement the only sound we could hear was him snoring.

"The shafoor usually has to carry the drunk gentleman to bed," she said. I had to give her credit, she was taking the mouse business very well. Beevers wasn't easy to get out of the car. Heavy? I bet he had to pay excess baggage on aeroplanes, quite apart from any luggage.

The air in the basement was just as stale as the air in the car but it was colder stale air. He recovered a bit as I was slow-waltzing him to the stairs. He mumbled and stumbled but he got his legs back. In fact, passing the desk he stopped to talk to the night bloke, a very tall geezer with a face like a side of bleached beef. "Got your Cup Final ticket upstairs, Tom," he managed to say.

"Thank you very much, Mr B, very grateful to you. Not the same on telly, is it?"

"Great great," Beevers growled.

I stopped and said, "Mr Beevers was wondering if a friend called for him on Thursday when they were out. Did the day blokes say anything?"

"George would have told me — no, he didn't mention it and I didn't see anybody."

"Okay, thanks."

Up in the flat she said she wanted to change and disappeared into their bedroom. He grabbed my arm and said we needed to have a private chat when she went to bed. He was still making sense but needed company to enjoy the bottle. Short of chopping his arm off I could hardly get out of it.

"It's only people with dull lives who like sleeping," he said.

I said just a small one so he lashed in a quadruple and shoved the cigars at me. I stretched back on a velvet chair and

141

caught a sight of the Post Office tower lights. "There should be an airfield under that thing," I said.

"What? What airfield? Listen, Jim — "

She came into the big lounge, still wearing the same outfit. Maybe it was her underwear needed changing. She said she would have a Cinzano. She sat on the sofa. Lucky old sofa. She caught me looking at her and gave me a brave little smile, just a helpless young lovely trapped in a scary situation she didn't understand.

That's what I was supposed to think anyway.

She pulled her legs up on to the sofa and adjusted the white gown to cover her knees. Her bare arm and shoulder were firm and smooth and tanned to the richness of golden syrup. She looked about as helpless as one of them female spiders who wraps up the enchanted evening with a quick snack of hot husband.

Beevers gave her the drink and plonked himself down on the other velvet chair. The china leopard stared disdainfully at a spot on the wall.

"I'm shattered," he said. "Why the bloody hell would anybody go to all this trouble?"

"We should get the police in — I'm getting frightened," she said, looking at me.

"You're not a bad judge as it happens," I said, looking at him, "this nutter is trying to tell you he can get at you any time he wants."

"We've nothing to show the police now," he mumbled. "Simone threw out the damaged clothes and we've probably wiped off the fingerprints. Anyway, no bloody fingerprints on a dead mouse, is there? To hell with the police, we'll handle this ourselves."

She put the back of her hand to her mouth. Even her armpit was smooth and tanned. It might have been a real yawn. She gave me a bright smile. I was sure she wasn't as innocent as her big brown eyes but that didn't stop me imagining my face sinking into the smooth warmth of her neck and shoulder.

"You should have some ointment on those cuts," she said, "they could turn septic."

I shrugged. "I gave 'em a bit of a scrubbing — "

"They'll be very nasty if they get inflamed."

She swung her legs off the sofa and went out of the lounge. Beevers stretched out at full length, holding his glass on his belly, breathing like a horse with asthma. Every time I looked at him I made a vow to take more exercise.

"I know I can trust you, Jim," he said. "No, I'm serious, I've been around a long time, there's not many I trust but you're all right — Jim, I said I didn't want the cops in because of Bert and the hit and run business — that wasn't the only reason, Jim, I got other problems — I'm surrounded by enemies, Jim, they all hate me, don't you think I *know*? They laugh at me behind my back, just a fat, ugly — "

"You'll feel better in the morning — "

"But I won't look any better, will I?"

I had to laugh. He started to pull himself upright. Some of the whisky spilled on his blue shirt. He did a bit of cursing and spluttering then forgot about sitting up. One of his trouser

144

legs was pulled halfway to his knee. He was wearing black socks with a suspender. Above the sock his skin was dead white and lumpy. "I'm not drunk," he snapped, "I never get drunk, I'm tired that's all, that stinking discotheque — "

She came striding into the lounge, the split gown making it look as if she was using only one long nyloned leg.

She had this little metal tube of ointment. I put out my hand to take it but she bent down to peer at my wounds.

When I looked up she was smiling about the eyes.

"Yes, very nasty," she said. She squeezed some white goo on to her middle finger and leaned close and started to rub it into my face. I couldn't see Beevers. Her knees were touching my thigh. Her bare arm stretched across my face, giving me a close-up of her smooth armpit.

I was surrounded by her. She went on rubbing. Her knees pressed harder on my thigh.

No doubt about it!

Next thing she put the back of her

145

hand against my lips! She smiled down at me, her eyes big and moist in the looming shadows of her face.

"You still may get some inflammation," she said quietly.

Then she put her red nails against my cheek and ran them down to my neck.

Inflamed? I should cocoa. Towering Infernos!

I crossed my legs sharpish as she stepped back but Beevers wasn't in any condition to spot the shape of things to come.

"I'm going to bed," she said. "Philip, you show Jim the spare room — you are staying the night, aren't you?"

"I'd better not — "

"Course you'll stay the night," Beevers said, waving his arm at the ceiling.

"I'm going to sleep in the small room, Philip," she said, "you always snore like a pig when you've been drinking."

"I am not drunk! What the hell gives you — "

She leant over and kissed his forehead. He grunted.

"I should push off home," I said, "got no toothbrush, have I?"

She laughed. "I would have thought you had to live dangerously in your job."

"That's why I need the ring of confidence."

I watched her bare brown back going through the door. Beevers sank deeper into the chair. "Bastards," he growled, "bastards, every bloody one of them."

Then he went a bit mad. He jumped up, spilling some more whisky on his trousers. He swayed a bit but managed it to the door. He closed it and went to the genuine antique cocktail cabinet and used the whisky bottle like a fireman's hose. Some of it got in the glass. He lumbered back and stood over me.

"All looks good from the outside, doesn't it?" he demanded, holding the glass at a tilt. I got ready to save myself from a whisky bath. Suddenly he shoved his right hand into his back pocket and brought out the big bundle. "I'm a fat ugly man, don't you think I know it?"

He chucked the bundle of readies at the china leopard. Its glass eyes reckoned the whole performance was pretty childish. He mumbled something and then aimed his big backside at the sofa. As he flopped down more whisky slopped on to his blue shirt. I don't think he even remembered I was present by then. He seemed to be speaking to somebody else, telling them not to worry, Philip Beevers would see off the lot of them, bastards that they were. His blinks got longer and longer and then his head went all the way back.

"My Mum always told me the rich ain't happy," I said. Silence. Then a snore. I put down my glass, which was still pretty full, and picked up his money and put it on the carved mantelpiece above the cold fireplace with the plastic logs. I let myself out on to the balcony.

It was all out there, the blackness of the park and the spaceship lights of the Post Office tower and the night that never really gets dark, the dull glow in the sky from all the lights in all the streets, the whole of London stretching away to the Surrey hills and the Thames mudflats, too big to understand.

What could you do?

Keep your head down in the noisy streets and make a few bob to see you through each day and try to kid yourself tomorrow would bring the answer?

It was cold out there in more ways than one so I went back into the lounge, leaving the doors open so the cold air might wake him up. She wasn't a bad judge about his snoring. He was flopped full-length on the sofa, one hand covering his nose and eyes. Poor Mr Beevers, I thought, lighting up one of his cigars and dropping into a big velvet chair, poor Mr Beevers.

Poor Mr Hazell, said another voice, what have you got to be boasting about?

Isn't it great — she says you're only quarter-educated so she'll give you good books to widen your horizons — you're definitely impressed that anybody as bright as her would fancy you — next thing you catch her in bed with the baby-face cousin?

The rich fat man went on snoring. Don't worry, Mr Beevers, we're all suffering one way or another.

★ ★ ★

The cold air woke him about half an hour later, still in a daze but steadier. He took

149

me along the corridor to the bedroom I'd been allocated. He showed me where the bathroom was. "Don't mind me, Jim," he said, "I talk a lot of crap when I'm pissed, see you in the morning."

"Yeah, good night, Mr Beevers, sleep tight and the bugs won't bite."

He lumbered off up the corridor. I went into the bathroom. It was something else. A black bath, marble maybe with little streaks of green among the black — and gold taps! I felt them to see if they were real gold.

They were cold and smooth. What does gold feel like anyway?

Luxury? A mother-of-pearl seat, clean towels on hot rails, a tiled shower compartment, a fitted carpet, fashion magazines on a little stool. I'm not joking, you could've enjoyed a fortnight's holiday in that bathroom.

What really got me was the seat flushing without a sound. I'd spent most of my life in places where you couldn't hear the radio if they pulled the chain six doors away. A silent flusher? Costs money that does.

In the bedroom I took off everything

150

150

and let my skin feel the cool, crisp sheets. Light blue they were, with matching pillows that weren't screwed into lumps like every pillow I've ever owned.

I switched off the bedside light.

Good night, Jim me old son, the lap of luxury at last.

* * *

If I'd been expecting trouble I could have crumpled up newspapers round the door like real detectives on television, only it wasn't trouble.

It was dangerous but it was no trouble.

She woke me by sliding in on top of me. Even in the dark I didn't have to ask for a name. There was only one body like that in the Beever's home — unless this Mrs O'Brien was a nudist hooverer.

9

HER hair was all over my face. Before I could scream or say something dramatic like Good gracious me she put her mouth on mine and slid her tongue in.

I pushed her face away.

"Are you easily shocked?" she said, quite loudly.

"Why, what do you do next?"

"I knew you wanted me as much as I wanted you."

"Does he know that you knew what I knew? I mean, you're taking a bit of a chance, aren't you?"

"He won't wake up. Anyway, I've locked his door."

"You've done *what*?"

I felt her body laughing. She had her knees pushed down between mine. "When I'm sleeping in the small room I always lock him in — he likes it."

"Like kinky you mean?"

"That's *nothing*. I'm sick of it. You're

not kinky, are you?"

"Only with women. Look, I hate to be a drag but I don't think this is a good idea."

"Why not? Don't you fancy me?"

Her hands started nipping and rubbing me, all over the shop they were. I reached up and pulled the light cord. She dropped her face on my chest. "Is this some kind of hint?" I said.

She peeked at me through her white-gold hair. She was laughing. I decided the clever thing was to go very gently without giving her any excuse for a neurotic fit.

Call me a naïve sentimental fool but wasn't it husbands who used to do the locking up?

"You know when I decided to do this?" she said, licking her finger-tip and rubbing a circle on my chest.

"Putting that ointment on my face — you felt my sense of romance stirring?"

"Before that. When you were driving us home. From the back you looked so big and tough — and capable. Up till then I'd thought of you as impossibly common."

"Flattered I'm sure. What do we do now then — ask Jason in to give me a grammar lesson?"

"Don't be silly."

"All right then — how about your friend Lou Nicholas?"

She frowned. "What is that supposed to mean?"

"I'm sure he could teach me a lot — how to be smooth and that."

Brown eyes in a blonde face, very healthy and innocent. "Don't let Lou's manner fool you. Just because he's got an Oxford accent doesn't mean he's soft. He's quite ruthless in fact."

"I've been to Oxford, you know, twice as it happens. Not so easy picking up the accent on day trips."

"You're quite droll at times." She ran her knuckles along my jaw. "I suppose you fool people into thinking you're a cockney moron with no brains then — wow!"

"Wow, I'm Brain of Britain?" I was trying to ease myself out from under but she was no featherweight. "I didn't think you'd go much on us common herberts — not from what Tony Manders was saying."

Her hands stopped moving. She lifted her head. "What did he tell you?"

"He says you're a bit of a tease but you don't go through with it. He also said you and your husband had a row because you were getting too pally with Nicholas. After that he told me wet weather makes his feet ache — "

"He's an oaf! Did he tell you I was giving *him* the come-on? What egos men have! Honestly — "

"Did you and Mr Beevers have a row about Nicholas?"

"For God's sake — surely you guess what it's like with Philip? He's eaten with jealousy, he thinks every man we meet is screwing me."

"I suppose he could get strange notions, men often do when you lock 'em up."

She got a bit annoyed at that. Her busy fingers turned into fists. I made a neat move and lifted her off and swung my legs off the edge of the bed and sat up.

She lay there on the inside, naked as sin and bold as brass. She was lightly tanned all over, no white bikini patches.

"Not your type am I?" she said sarcastically.

155

"What's it all about, Jim, I keep asking myself."

"I don't see anything strange in this. Can't a woman simply decide she'd like to have a certain man and then do something about it?"

"Some are more subtle than others about it."

"You *are* shocked! How very amusing."

"I was brainwashed with stupid conventions I expect."

"My God. It's all right for men to make a grab at everything in sight but not for women?"

"It is a bit different for men."

"You don't seriously — " she stared at me with her big brown eyes, then she snorted with laughter. "You're nothing but an old-fashioned male chauvinist! All right for men but not for women? My God — "

"There's also the little matter of your husband. He isn't paying me good money to come into his home and look for clues in bed with his wife, is he?"

I thought I was doing a good line in talking her out of the whole idea.

Then I felt her nails on my spine. I

looked round. She was blowing me a little kiss.

"Anyway, while we've got a moment," I said "you sure you got no idea who's pulling these strokes? They all seem to be aimed at you, wouldn't you say?"

"Yes — and I'm very, very frightened."

"You look about as frightened as Desperate Dan." She had a firmer body than you would have thought from her soft face. Her thighs were long and brown. Her bristols were a proper pair, like a real bosom.

"Can I ask you one simple question? Are you and Lou Nicholas having it off?"

"Next question."

I flopped on the bed and leaned on my elbow. "It's all right, I won't be comparing notes with him."

Her eyes went narrow and she drew in a sharp hiss. We glared at each other from close range.

"If you were so keen on the cops why didn't you ring 'em soon as you found your gear covered in paint?"

"I knew Philip didn't want the police involved."

"Oh? The obedient little wife already? Why doesn't he want to risk the cops?"

"He's evading income tax."

"And where money's involved nothing else matters, eh? Always interested me that has — you marry a geezer for his loot, do you both admit it to each other when you're alone? I mean — "

Her eyes tried to murder me. "I didn't marry him for his money," she snapped. "I had the money, he was almost bankrupt! I was married before, my husband left me, I got a fifty-thousand pound house in Gerrards Cross under the settlement. All he had was a furniture importing business that wasn't worth twopence. Did he tell you I married him for his money? The rotten swine — "

"Straight up?"

"We'll go and ask him right now."

"Charming thought, the two of us bollock-naked steam into his locked bedroom and say — here, mush, give us a butcher's at yer bankbook!"

She was twisting away from me by then.

"So why did you marry him then? Love was it?"

"You cynical shit! He didn't tell me he was broke until afterwards. My first husband was too young, I suppose I was looking for security, a father-figure — if that's an expression you would know."

"Yeah well, I never had no father-figure, only a Dad. But he's got plenty of loot now, hasn't he?"

"With my capital he got off to a new start — then he had to get mixed up with Lou bloody Nicholas."

"You don't like Nicholas then?"

"Like him?" She almost spat. "I loathe and despise him. He *disgusts* me."

"Yeah? You looked quite matey tonight."

"There's something like twenty-five thousand pounds of our money tied up in the partnership. Until we see how to get it back we have to play friends with him. We're in a very awkward situation. Now will you let me go?"

"Hang about — you mean you really did fancy me?"

She pouted "I was *terribly* mistaken."

"No, it was me who made the mistake. Still, not too late, is it?"

"Oh yes it is." She tried to jump up. I

put my hand against the wall. She tried to slide down under my arm. I got a hold of her behind the knees and pulled her back up on to the pillow. I kissed her arm and then her shoulder and then her neck. She tasted of flowers. She hissed something and tried to push my chest away. I smiled down at her. She slapped my face. I blew her a little kiss. She tried to knee me down below.

"You know the way to a man's heart, don't you?" I said. I crushed down on top of her. She lay still for a moment. I stroked her hair. She wriggled a bit.

Suddenly it was all happening again. Everywhere I went her skin was a thrill to touch. Of course it was all a mistake — downright perverted with him locked up two doors down the corridor.

Still, there you go.

She wrapped herself round me and all the aches and bruises vanished in the magic madness, in the single bed, just one little room from all the thousands and thousands of rooms under the night glare of the big cold city, just a few moments of magic.

Her small voice in the dark. "You don't really think somebody is planning to do something awful to me, do you? I'm so frightened at times."

"Not frightened now, are you?"

"How can you find out who's doing these things?"

"You've already given me new clues. If we stay in bed for a week we'll end up solving the Jack the Ripper case. You can tell me now — between friends — do this sort of thing often, do you?"

Silence.

Then, "I've had one or two lovers, yes. Can you blame me?"

"But not Lou Nicholas? He looks as if he's got the boilings for you."

"For every woman you mean. He's like a snake, always sliding up behind you and touching your bum — ugh! I bet he keeps a diary and awards himself points. Of course, like most of that type he basically hates women."

"I don't suppose you'd tell me any other names."

"No, I would not. Anyway, none of

161

them would do anything horrible to me."

"I'll bet they wouldn't. Mrs Beevers, the golden girl — "

"I'm going now — "

"Oh no you're not. Basically I like women — been my trouble all along."

"Let me go!"

"You shouldn't start anything you can't finish, Mrs Golden Girl . . . "

★ ★ ★

He came into the bedroom about nine. He was in a long silk dressing-gown over light-blue pyjamas. His dyed hair wasn't combed properly and he looked a bit like an old woman. He had a cup of tea and six biscuits on a little blue plate.

Honest to God, I wanted to apologize.

"Sleep okay?" he said.

"Smashing."

"I've got a touch of the iron turbans — sorry if I got a bit overwrought last night, few drinks, you know how it is. Like a big breakfast, do you?"

"Whatever's going. Here, while I remember — when are you getting

162

that lock changed?"

"The bloke came and did it yesterday, didn't I tell you?"

"That was quick."

"The mention of a few extra quid generally cuts a lot of corners." He went to the window. Without his tailoring he looked a lot older and baggier. His ankles were white and skinny. I sucked in some tea and toyed with a biscuit or two, gulp gulp.

"Might stay dry for the Cup Final," he said, "I'm really looking forward to it, aren't you? Everton can't hope to win the Cup playing negative stuff — and Sheffield United play an open game. I should think it'll be a cracker. Good seats we've got — ten pounds — cost me four times that of course but still."

"I'll be watching it on telly — "

"No, you're coming with us. We'll have my partner with us — "

"You mean you've got a ticket for me?"

"I usually buy about fifty, Jim, spread 'em round people for business reasons. Listen, when these people come — "

"What people's that, Mr Beevers?"

"Phil, please, sounds so formal. I always have a few friends in for a glass of champagne before the Wembley final, almost an annual ritual. Stay in bed as long as you like."

"I better get home and change first, I've been in these socks for two days."

"I'll give you a pair — "

"Thanks but I might have some urgent mail."

"Well, be back here soon as you like."

"About the other business — "

He gave me a little grimace. "I was hoping we could forget that just for today, I'd so like to enjoy the Cup Final without that cropping up. Just enjoy yourself, Jim."

I had my tea and got up and managed to reach the bath room without being seduced or given more surprise treats.

He cooked the breakfast!

She didn't even get up! By the time I realized he was doing the housework it was too late to say I didn't want any. I sat at the glass and steel table in the tiled kitchen and wolfed down what was on the plate, four sausages, two slices of bacon, a fried egg, a fried tomato, a rack of toast and coffee. When I'd whacked that lot into me he was gone so I said "Be back shortly" into the empty corridor and headed for the lift.

When it opened out came three blokes and a woman carrying cardboard boxes and square metal containers. I stood back and then said, "Here — that wouldn't be for Mr Beevers, would it?"

"That's right, sir."

"Oh yeah?" I let the door slide to. "Who're you from?"

"Fraser Catering."

I went back with them to the shiny black door. Had to be another hoax, didn't it?

Beevers opened the door. There were a few tufts of soap on his neck. He was carrying a towel the way men do when they're caught shaving, holding it under his chin in case his face intended to slide off.

"Look what's turned up," I said, showing him the four people with the boxes, "seems like Mr X has struck again — "

165

"Fraser's is it?" he said to them. "Come in, I'll show you where it all has to go." They filed into the flat, giving me funny looks.

"You mean you did order all that?" I said.

"Just bits and pieces for the snacks."

"Who've you asked — the whole Wembley crowd?"

He smiled. "Don't be long, Jim. By the way, I'm going to have a word with George downstairs about keeping an eye out for gate-crashers."

Well well.

No wonder the country was broke, these people had collared all the money.

I gave George at the desk a nice good morning and he sort of grunted. I caught a cab in Prince Albert Road and asked him for Hertford Street where I'd left the motor before going to the Hilton. Soon as we hit the West End you could tell it was Cup Final day, little armies of Everton and Sheffield supporters enjoying a butcher's at all this sophisticated London glamour before hitting the Wembley trail.

When two groups passed each other

they would let out the usual war-cries and hold their scarves above their heads. "Always wonder myself what your tourists make of all that shouting," the cabbie said. "I mean, gotta look strange, hundreds of people chanting and waving scarves in the air?"

"Maybe they think we do it all the time."

"Watching it on the tube, are yer?"

"Got a ten pound seat as it happens."

"You can get a hundred for that."

"Nah, not the same on telly."

"Better I think, mind you it's only my opinion like, few beers, git the old woman outa the house, couple me mates in, not saying it isn't a great atmosphere like, live and that, but more comfortable, innit? Better view into the bargain."

"Yeah?"

When I got out he squinted at me and said, "Here, you're not a footballer, are yer?"

"No, I'm a private detective."

He laughed like a drain. As he was fishing for change I saw the Cellophane envelope on my windscreen.

"Of all the poxy — cor, they been up

early, they've slapped a ticket on me already."

"They got an all-night team now, hunney."

"Traffic wardens on the bleeding night shift? Jesus Christ."

"Private detective," he said, shaking his head at the jollity of it all. He was still laughing as he shot off. I got in the Stag and headed for Ravenscourt Park by way of Park Lane, Bayswater Road and Shepherd's Bush Green. It was a dull grey day with a bit of a breeze. After the heat of the Beevers's mansion flat I felt more healthy with the window down. Shepherd's Bush looked shabby but normal — you can see people's faces better when there isn't a ton of money between you. Call me a naïve sentimental fool but a lot of the time I wish I had an ordinary job and a nice wife buying the grub in the supermarket while I'm standing outside with the pram.

There was only one letter for me. It didn't have a stamp. I opened it as I went upstairs to the two rooms and bathroom I didn't call home, just a place to keep the rain off when I'd nowhere better to sleep.

I took the transistor into the bathroom and gave the Ascot geyser a bang to get hot water running into the crummy bath with the brown stains.

The letter was no great shock. The woman who owned the house, Mrs Nordstrom, wanted me out. It was from her solicitors, cheap notepaper from the kind of legal giants who operate in the old grocery shop between the sick animals' dispensary and the betting shop. Being as how it was furnished accommodation and the landlady lived on the premises I had no security of tenure under law. They suggested three months' notice. Just goes to show, you can't live on premises.

In the bath I listened to the commercial channel where news comes first, after the adverts. Same news as always, big unions wanting big rises, politicians calling each other scoundrels, doom all round and national bankruptcy in two minutes.

What was I doing in a nowhere place like Ravenscourt Park anyway? Must be a million better areas in this thrilling big city. Colossal rents, of course, maybe this time I should *buy* a flat with central heating and a decent bath and get a colour set and a hi-fi to play lulling music while I gave the business to Miss Right.

There had to be a Miss Right somewhere, didn't there?

I knocked on Mrs Nordstrom's door on my way out. She looked embarrassed when I held up the solicitor's letter.

"I'm sorry about it, Mr Hazell, it's my daughter, she has two children and her husband has left her and one of the little ones has to be near a hospital for remedial treatment and she has nowhere else to go — "

"That's all right, Mrs Nordstrom, I'll find somewheres else soon as I can. I'll let you know next week maybe."

"You're sure you don't mind? I really am very sorry about this, Mr Hazell, you've been no trouble, I wouldn't have done this for the world but my daughter is desperate and — "

"Yeah, I understand, don't worry."

She said I was a brick.

At least I hoped she said brick.

Her gratitude made me feel like a Boy Scout for five minutes. Then it was back to the money people.

★ ★ ★

A few hours before life was dodgy for the Beevers but it was all go now behind the shiny black door on the seventh floor. A few friends in for a glass of champagne he'd said. I counted fifty before my fingers got cramp, most of them your paunchy generation trying to hide it all behind snazzy blazers and six-guinea hairstyles.

"Get yourself some nosh, Jim," said Beevers, pointing me towards the caterers' table where a little queue was waiting, plates in hand, the geezer in the white jacket slapping on a slice of this and a leg of that and a dollop of doings. Cold buffet you'd call it.

She looked in, Simone, the golden girl with the lisp to starboard. She was in a white trouser suit with high-heeled yellow shoes and a silk scarf round her lovely gregory. Her hair was done up with a black bow at the back. She gave me a quick look and then sailed on past to say hullo to Lou Nicholas and friend.

I knew it wasn't something we could've

171

made an announcement about but I did think she might have smiled.

Beevers stood beside me for a moment. "Knows how to pick 'em does our Lou," he said cheerfully, admiring his partner's bird, a black girl in a black leather suit, the shiny kind that looks like inky skin. "She's a singer — lousy voice but who's listening?"

"One look at her and Enoch Powell's singing Bingo Bango Bongo I don't wanna leave the Congo!"

He laughed. A big man with a big bundle and a million friends, that was Phil Beevers, in daylight.

Nicholas gave me a slight nod and took his spade bird through to the lounge. Beevers said, "Have some champers, Jim, tuck in, good times are just around the corner."

"Unless you're facing the wrong direction in a one-way street."

He patted me on the shoulder. "Let's just enjoy today, Jim, eh? I just want to forget it all for an hour or two. Thing like this — puts a black cloud over everything, doesn't it? You look at all your friends and you think — do I really

172

know the truth about *anybody*?"

He put his hand to his forehead as if to get a grip of a headache. Then he smiled and dived off into the excitement.

I felt sorry for him, just at that moment. There didn't seem to be any actual people in his life, just mouths and hands, the mouths saying how much, the hands flexing to shake his money.

On the other hand, I could afford to feel sorry for him, I'd been paid in advance.

Through the door came Young Mister Smooth himself, Paul Shirriff no less, wearing a light grey suit, black rollneck sweater and black boots. On his arm was a black leather coat. As he was parking the coat I got hold of Beevers's arm. "How much does Shirriff know?"

"Everything — up till the paint anyway."

"You want him to know about the rest of it?"

"Why not? He's a friend."

Shirriff came my way from the buffet table, a healthy load on his plate. "So — you took the job then," he said.

173

"Yeah — thanks for shoving it my way."

"You were the best man for the job, that's all." He watched Beevers slapping some people on the back. "He's a soft touch, old Phil," he murmured, "his friends have to look after his interests."

"You ain't doing too badly I notice — what's that you've got on your plate, the first three-winged chicken?"

As I say, you could not needle Paul Shirriff.

"One of the most generous people I know, old Phil," he said.

"Close friends are you?"

"I first bumped into him last year, we were handling security for an open-air pop festival they put on up Norfolk way."

A waiter in a white jacket came round with a bottle in every hand. Shirriff emptied his glass to make room for a new lot. We were shoulder to shoulder, like spectators, not looking at each other. "I gave you a ring yesterday," he said. "I couldn't get any joy from your office number."

"Working on this job, wasn't I?"

174

"What happens to potential clients if they can't get in touch?"

"Their fingers start walking through the yellow pages again I expect. Do me a favour — don't start all that crap about a partnership."

"It's not crap. You know my position. National Security operates under the dead hand of the Webb family, I've gone as far up their career structure as any outsider is allowed to go. God, the ideas they turn down — for no reason at all. This whole field is wide open, nobody trusts the majority of the rascals and hustlers who call themselves private detectives. My idea is to set up a solid, respectable basis, maybe hire a few types away from Scotland Yard while they're still in their prime, sell ourselves on the concept of — "

"And end up just as bloody boring to work for as National Security Systems?"

"But where are you going on your own?"

"The toilet, now you mention it."

On my way back I looked in the lounge. It was pretty full, businessmen and their wives, a few young trendies.

175

A well-known disc jockey was rabbiting away to Lou Nicholas and his glamour-girl. Shirriff was talking to Simone. He said something witty and she laughed, throwing back her head, lovely neck. Maybe he was offering her some concept or another.

"You look too sober," she said when I came up, "why don't you relax?"

"I'll take a relaxative."

She went off to say mahvellous to six other people. I lit a fag and put the match back in the box.

"Bit early for grinding them into the Persian rugs," I said catching him giving me a funny look.

"About Phil's little problem — what do you know about the state of the parties between him and Lou Nicholas?"

"Not a lot."

"Well don't quote me — but as one professional to another — my opinion is that Nicholas is one hundred per cent flannel."

"He says ninety per cent."

"He's full of bullshit about his big plans to turn them into an entertainment conglomerate but nothing ever seems to come to much. We got paid for that Norfolk fiasco but we were in a very small minority."

"So he's full of crap. Where's the angle for him to start playing silly hoaxes?"

"I'm not saying it is Nicholas — I'm just saying the situation might be worth investigating. Phil's naïve in many ways. Very hard world behind all the jolly gladhanding, show business."

"Be grateful we're in a gentleman's racket then. 'Scuse me a moment."

I found Beevers with the disc-jockey and a couple of furniture dealers. They were saying a decent spring cruise should be on the National Health, for businessmen. The disc-jockey was wondering if Portugal would ever be a safe bet for holidays again. His newspaper photos didn't show his bad acne. To cure it he'd been giving himself sun-lamp treatment, one of those tans your nails could peel off from the neck. All he'd really managed was give himself an orange acne.

I gave Beevers a nod and he came with me to the big windows.

"I'm going to give the flat a quick

tour if you don't mind," I said, "all this could be a good cover for another little caper."

He stared out over the park. "Whatever you say, Jim. We'll be leaving for Wembley in about half an hour."

"Yeah well, cheer up, probably he's done his worst."

"If I could only believe that . . . "

I slid off into the corridor. The bathroom was occupied. The catering lady was washing dishes in the shiny kitchen. My bedroom was exactly the way I'd left it, although somebody had made the bed. Not Beevers, I hoped. What a horrible thought!

The next room was occupied by Jason the fashion hound. The sweet smell of Kennel Number Five. I've never seen a special dog's room before. It had straw matting and a basket big enough to manage a family of four for a boating holiday.

Jason was chewing a red rubber bone. He gave me a casual glance and let his tail flop once on the floor.

"If you need anything just woof," I said. He ignored me.

The Beevers's white and gold bedroom was okay and the small adjoining bedroom, the one she used on snoring nights, was full of coats.

Coming out of it I met a familiar face. He half-knew me, too. We frowned cheerfully at each other for a moment. The party in the lounge was getting noisier. He was a round-shouldered geezer, quite big, with a teenager's fringe and foxy eyes.

"You're the Old Bill," he said accusingly, looking at me sideways.

"Ex. I know your collar from somewheres?"

"Who — *me*? Nah, must be some other ice-cream who looks like me, Gawd help him." He gave me a wink and went into the lounge.

Shirriff got hold of me again. "Phil tells me you stayed the night here," he said. Half of his mouth was threatening to smile. "Simone's rather lovely, isn't she?" The other half of his mouth was trying to leer. He would have needed a safety net to smile outright.

"That supposed to mean something?"

He gave me a little nudge. "They're

all doing it in these circles, you know."

"Picking their noses and chewing it?"

"Come on now — " he gave me the naughty-naughty look, "I know Simone. Phil got a bit pie-eyed, didn't he? Left you two alone, no?"

"Yeah but Jason wouldn't go to bed. What the hell are you getting at, Shirriff?"

He gave me a wink. Beevers came across.

"There's only one secret to living," he told us, sounding as if the news had just been flashed on the screen, "simple really but few people cotton on till it's too late — enjoy every minute because you'll never get that particular minute back again."

"How true, Phil," said Shirriff. I couldn't tell if he was taking the micky. The new plastic man, nobody knows what he's thinking, the world's going to be full of them in a minute, *Leggo* men, every piece interchangeable. Maybe he wasn't thinking anything at all. I was thinking — you're earning good money here, Jim, don't knock it.

Around quarter to two Beevers went to

the end of the lounge where the biggest group was watching the pre-match stuff on the colour set. He cleared his throat and raised his hands. Just for a moment he looked ready to start tap-dancing.

"Well, boys and girls," he announced, "them that's going to the game better think about making a move. The rest of you — please wire into the grub, plenty of champers left."

"How many aren't coming?" I said as we headed for the door.

"I dunno, quite a few — it's all right, Jim, Simone will have plenty of people to look after her. We're taking Lou and Barbara."

"What's the name of that geezer in the brown cardigan jacket?" I said, looking at the round-shouldered bloke who'd remembered me from the police.

"Oh that's Danny Aldous, he's the source for the tickets, one of Lou's blokes actually — bit of a crook if you ask me."

"You're not wrong. Danny Aldous — yeah. I've met him. One of your bookshop team is he?"

"Him and a bloke called Tommy

Ableman run that side of it more or less. You know him?"

"As you say, Mr Beevers, does anyone really know anybody?"

"That's the way things are in this world — let's pretend it's all for real, just for today, eh?"

Lou Nicholas, the spade girl, name of Barbara, Beevers and me went down in the lift with two of his business friends, all a bit giggly with the champagne. I'd assumed we were travelling in the Rolls but no — waiting in the basement was an Austin Princess limousine, with driver, a smallish bloke of about fifty in a black suit with a shafoor's cap. "Fryatt Cars — for Beevers?" said Beevers.

"Yes, sir."

Beevers was wearing a sheepskin coat that made him big enough to sprint a measured mile round. "Is this your party, sir? We should get going, traffic will be heavy."

He held the door for us. Barbara got in first. She had a full-length fur coat over her leather suit. She was one of those who isn't ashamed of the frizzy hair, in fact she had enough of it to keep the snow off the cabbages. Bingo bango bongo!

Lou Nicholas got in next. He was wearing a fawn alpaca coat, pearl grey suit and suede boots. He was smoking four inches of thin black cheroot.

Beevers wanted me to get in next but I didn't want to be close to Nicholas so I took the jump seat, just behind the driver. Big car that, easily room for five standing downstairs, but the others looked crushed beside the big bulk of Beevers in the sheepskin coat.

They knew clever ways to get to Wembley, missing most of the traffic. Beevers did most of the talking, telling us what a great game it was going to be, occasionally leaning forward to tell the driver things he knew already. She didn't know anything about football and didn't say much at all, except when they started talking about people they knew in the wonderful mahvellous world of show biz.

Lou Nicholas was the kind who makes you wonder what went wrong with his happy childhood. Every time Beevers mentioned a name he put the knock in. Anywhere Beevers or the girl had been he'd been there earlier before it was spoiled.

He didn't use too many words but they'd all been sharpened to an edge.

Didn't offer me one of his cigars either. Matter of fact he more or less treated me as being something to do with the driver.

Why mess about, he was a shit.

Then we hit Wembley Park tube station and the big crowds on the road up to Wembley Stadium, Olympic Way, a broad avenue with trees, on a big match day just about the most exciting street in London, half the population of England marching towards the twin domes of the stadium, the big flags flying, the shouting of the popcorn blokes and the newsvendors and the ice-cream salesmen and the blokes opening up the human sea to let through the big official motors, maybe a sight of the team buses if you're there early enough.

"You'd have done better to wear flat-heeled shoes," I said to Barbara, thinking we were going to get out and walk.

"Driver — to the top and then into

the car-park on the left," said Beevers.

"Yes, sir."

"Isn't that for official cars only?" I was dumb enough to say. Nicholas sneeringly put me right.

"In a car like this very few people will try to interfere," he said.

He was wrong as it happened.

Beevers must've had these kinds of ambitions all his life, to play Flash Harry in front of the sweaty soccer masses, but it began to look as if he was fated to be Muggins no matter how hard he worked at being Mr Big.

10

THE first lot who spotted the beautiful Barbara were from Sheffield. The Austin Princess was making ground through the crowds at the speed of a tortoise with time on its hands.

First off they started tapping the windows, a dozen or so of them in team scarves and rosettes, just touching the windows and leering politely.

"Nice enough blokes in their own homes I expect," I said, "only big games have this strange effect on the quietest people."

"Bloody oafs," Beevers muttered, keeping a smile on his face.

Then it was a bunch from Liverpool, all togged up in Everton blue, some of them wearing top hats with blue and white stripes. As you'd expect from Scouses they were a bit livelier. Even with the windows shut we could hear various remarks, mainly to do with various uses the spade bint could be put to. Noses were pressed against glass.

"Always wondered what a goldfish felt like," I said.

"It's all right, my dear, they're pretty good-natured these Scouses," Beevers said to Barbara. Nicholas blew cigar smoke at the ceiling. Faces were only inches away from us through the glass, the sort of English faces that don't get to ride in limousines, spotty faces, fat faces, unshaven faces, toothless faces, twisted faces, brown teeth, long hair that needed washing, bright anoraks, jeans, one or two showing off their muscles by only wearing sleeveless Fair Isle pullovers, all of them making jokes and gestures and us sitting there like dummies in our big warm car.

"Prince Philip would know better how to handle this," I said. Nicholas sneered.

"Our masters the public." Suddenly I was on the side of those blokes outside.

Worse was to come. That first lot had tickets. Halfway up towards the twin domes we attracted about thirty Everton teenagers without briefs. The big car and the big fat man with the sheepskin coat and the slim dark man with the cigar and the black girl added up to just about everything those kids were never going to get.

They banged on the windows with the flat of their hands. They surrounded the car and started to chant. Then they banged on the roof.

"Got any spurr tickets, Mister?" they shouted through the glass. For some reason they all seemed to pick on Beevers. I kind of sat there, looking at the back of the driver's head and hoping I looked like some bum who'd got a lift.

Beevers stared ahead, hardly moving his lips as he told the driver to hurry it up.

"I'm trying my best, sir, I might run over one of them," said the little man in the black peaked cap.

"Run over six of them," said Nicholas.

The banging on the roof grew louder. One of the bleeders climbed on the boot. Noses flattened on glass until we couldn't see out for faces.

The inside of the car went dark as each window became a wall of human features, all grinning at us something diabolical.

I cannot tell a lie, I was near to getting out of the motor and walking away. Those kids were spot on, we were the smart boys London is famous for, well-dressed spivs who get all that's going and sneer at naïve punters who sweat their guts out in the black-pudding belt.

"Ugly-looking swine, aren't they?" said Nicholas, smiling sarcastically at some fifteen-year-old with a brass-studded denim jacket and the face of a college boy. He got his mouth against the glass and yelled, "She any good in fookin bed, Mister?" He put his hand on his biceps and shoved his fist up and down. Eton maybe.

"Got any spurr tickets?" they kept shouting.

Then they started to rock the car.

All this was being watched by the armies walking on either side of us but why should any of them risk a hammering to help some smarmy toffs in a big limousine?

Barbara giggled nervously. Nicholas went on smoking his cigar.

Beevers gave her knee a pat. "Only

their high spirits," he said.

"Why doesn't that mountie chase them away?" Nicholas said tetchily. A shiny black boot in a stirrup passed the window. The boys hung back until the crowds behind swallowed up the copper.

The banging took up again.

"Yeah well, they follow these teams through rain and snow and then they don't get tickets for the Cup Final, only natural they think something's wrong somewhere," I said. "No ticket for you, Jack, the seats have all been snapped up by fur coats and cigars who wouldn't know a free kick from a dose of fowl pest."

"Give them your ticket then," Nicholas snapped.

"Don't be silly," said Beevers, still smiling.

As soon as we turned on to the big cinder parking area we were stopped by a white rope and two attendants with official bands on their arms.

"Official passes only," the little driver said.

"Nonsense!" Beevers moved very quickly, out of the car and striding towards the two attendants, his right hand diving under the sheepskin coat. He got up close to the two blokes and they all started rabbiting away at each other.

"That's the only official pass you need," Nicholas said, "gets you in anywhere."

"I often do wonder if there's anybody can't be straightened, know what I mean?" I said.

"Everybody's got their price."

Beevers turned and waved us to come on up. One of the attendants lifted away the rope.

He got back in the car, panting a bit.

"Up there to the very top, driver," he ordered. Then he gave us all an important smile. "Nothing to it," he said.

We parked behind five other limousines, all in a row pointing the same way. A bunch of chauffeurs were already getting together in a little cluster, swopping gossip about their bosses.

"Come on, we don't want to miss all the pre-match atmosphere," Beevers said. "Driver — we'll probably be out five minutes early so don't wander away, will you?"

"No sir, I'll be here."

Once away from the car I felt I could breathe again, although with Barbara in tow we weren't too anonymous.

As we came up on to the promenade behind the stand blokes were rushing here and there at rumours of a ticket for sale. Desperate men, willing to fork out a month's wages just to see their team in the game of a lifetime. Sliding about in the crowds were the slippery touts, doing quick deals and then moving off, always six or seven blokes arriving just too late and the one who'd bought the ticket pushing away quickly before anybody could snatch it.

"See that?" Beevers turned, his face excited. "Bloke just paid fifty quid for a terracing ticket!"

"There's one born every minute and here they all are in bulk," Nicholas said.

"He'll remember the game long after the fifty quid," I remarked. Barbara just kept smiling at everything.

We went up the stairs and Beevers

produced our four bits of stiff paper that people down there would have sold their souls for. Honest to God, I was embarrassed.

At last Barbara remembered a bit of conversation.

"It's almost as bad as Frank Sinatra's farewell concert," she said. "Were you there?"

"No, I'm waiting for his next farewell concert."

"I need a drink," Nicholas said.

"Suit yourself, I want to enjoy the atmosphere," Beevers said. Nicholas took Barbara through to the big crowded bar. Beevers and I went up the steps and out into the open stadium. You could have flown a cement kite on the noise. He stood there and shook his head.

"Fantastic. Isn't it just *fantastic*, Jim?"

"Terrific."

He took a grip of my arm. "Just ignore that bastard Lou. I wish I could have given their tickets to some of those kids back there. He doesn't even like football. Not fair, is it?"

He gave me a little guilty smile and we went where the steward pointed. The noise was incredible, Sheffield fans in red and white at one end, Everton blue at the other. You couldn't hear the military band for the mass roars, the singing of *You'll never walk alone*, the staccato barking of the team's names, louder and louder, the grass so green it looked like a colour set with the brilliance too high, the pigeons sweeping under the big roof that goes right round the stadium, the messages coming up on the electric scoreboard.

"Just incredible," Beevers said when we got to our seats. We were surrounded by the camel-hair coat, every bookie in London by the look of it, metal hip-flasks and ten-inch Coronas, enough peroxide to bleach Epping Forest.

Then the teams came out. The noise must have reached outer space, the two managers walking in front of the lines, the radio-cameramen running backwards in front, a hundred thousand mad people making a din you could have put in bottles.

As it happened it wasn't the greatest Cup Final in history. It never is. When Sheffield got their third goal about ten minutes from the end none of us had any objection when Beevers said we should get away before the crowd.

At the turnstiles a gate-man was letting a few Sheffield boys in to see the last few minutes. They ran like hell across the big dark corridor. Beevers looked tired. "Thanks a lot, Phil," I said, "I really appreciated it."

"A pleasure, Jim."

Nicholas showed us his half ticket. "Ninety minutes ago it was worth two hundred. So what was all the fuss about?" He skimmed the ticket across the floor. Beevers gave me a look. He'd been telling me during the game how he'd started watching Fulham forty-five years before, when he was only seven. Mad about the game he was. It made him less artificial. I suppose we all used to see those big cars taking the nobs to football matches and wish we were in them. The difference was he'd actually done it.

"Let's hope that little twit is ready to go," he said as we hurried across the promenade, past the dejected groups who'd come all that way just to hear the roars from the lucky ones inside.

The driver was ready all right. He was waiting beside the big black bonnet of the Austin Princess. He was ready to weep.

"Good God!" said Beevers.

Half the windscreen had gone. Big splinters were still sliding off the broken edges. Small fragments covered the shiny paintwork like broken ice in a gutter.

"What the hell happened?" Beevers demanded.

"Somebody threw a brick," the little man said, looking at us for sympathy, "I was only — "

"Who threw a brick?"

"I didn't see it. I was having a cup of tea with the other drivers at the stall down there — "

"Jesus Christ!"

"You didn't see them?" I said.

"No, we was all down there at the tea-stall, we heard the shattering, when we got up it was like this — about ten minutes ago. Nobody saw it."

"Any of these other cars damaged?"

"No, just this one."

I went up the line to where three or four chauffeurs were having a smoke. "Any of you blokes see who chucked

196

the brick?" I asked.

"Nah, be kids, just hooligans," one of them said.

Beevers was waving at me. I went back down the line. They were still roaring inside the stadium. "He can drive if he goes slow," he said. He looked very pale.

I helped the driver to lift most of the broken bits off the bonnet, trying not to scratch the paintwork. Nicholas stood well back, ignoring us, too superior to get involved. The girl could only frown. I got the brick from the floor of the car and smacked out most of the broken triangles still in the frame. The half that hadn't been knocked out was snow white with cracks.

We all got in the back and off we went, only this time we didn't look so flash. The crowds streaming down Olympic Way to the tube station all had a good point-up at the smashed windscreen and the driver's frightened little face peering through the big hole. They all thought it was very funny.

Beevers was licking at his moustache and beard again. She looked scared.

Nicholas seemed bored by the whole thing.

The driver made a little groan as we turned up on to the main road. He put his left hand to his eye and the big car wobbled a bit.

"There's bits falling into my face with the wind," he explained.

"Bloody freezing in here," said Nicholas, "tell him to put up the partition, Phil."

"Driver — can you put up the partition, we're turning to blocks of ice back here."

The driver pressed a button and thick glass rose up slowly and silently and the wind couldn't reach us.

"We ought to stop and knock the rest of the glass out," I said, "bits are getting in his face — "

"If he'd stayed with the car it wouldn't have happened," Nicholas snapped.

Beevers hardly said a word the whole way back to Regent's Park, just stared out of the window and licked his beard.

When we got out of the limousine at Inverson Court the little driver looked colder than a bucket of fish. I wasn't too sorry for him. Driving with glass dust in his eyes and a gale round his earholes and a bunch of chancers keeping warm in the back? He deserved a chill.

Give Beevers credit, he got out the big bundle and loomed over the little bloke as he thumbed a couple of notes off the top.

The little twit touched his cap!

★ ★ ★

As we came into the foyer George Jobsworth got to his feet and held out a brown envelope. "A lad dropped this in for you, Mr B. Enjoy your match?"

"Yes, very good afternoon." I looked over his shoulder. It was a plain brown envelope. On the front was typed *P. Beevers Esq* and in the top left corner, *Personal — by Hand*.

"Hurry up, you'll miss the bus," Nicholas called cheerily from the lift doors. Beevers ripped off the end of the envelope. "Come on, Phil," Nicholas shouted.

"You go on up, I'll be with you in a minute," Beevers said quietly. He turned his back on the desk. Then he handed the sheet to me. It was typed, in black, very neat lines.

Now you know we can get to you when we like. Impressed?
We know what business you are in and why you cannot yell for the boys in blue. We want £15,000 in cash — you don't want your lovely young wife to suffer worse than mice and paint, do you?
Someone will phone you soon and tell you where to deliver the money.
                                    A Friend

As soon as we were in the lift he started to cry, silent tears at first and then big heaving sobs.

11

"WHAT business are you really in?" I said a bit testily.

He got a grip of himself and wiped his eyes with a big blue hankie. "I'm terrified, Jim, I can't help it. When I saw that windscreen I couldn't believe it!"

"The windscreen?" I frowned. "You got more to worry about than that, Mr Beevers."

"Oh Jesus, Jim, what the hell's happening? What am I going to do?"

We walked along the warm corridor. He kept sniffing. "If I knew the score I could maybe help you," I said.

He shrugged.

There were still a dozen or so people in the lounge. It was full of smoke. The astrays were spilling over and dirty glasses were choc-a-bloc on the shiny antique furniture. It felt a bit nasty, like coming out of the cinema into sunshine.

I went to the kitchen for a glass of

water. My mouth was sore from all the fags I'd been smoking. My face felt tired. I used the toilet in the five-star bathroom and washed up and went back to the lounge. Simone was seeing off a couple of guests but there were still half a dozen or so watching the Cup Final goals on the box — well, they could only have shown them ten times.

I let myself out on the balcony. It was a grey afternoon. London was a dead, grey place. Come to that, I was a dead, grey place. Was I going to spend the rest of my life with strangers, people with whom the only thing I had in common was their money?

Beevers closed the french doors and put his elbows beside mine on the ledge.

"This is for all you've done, Jim, thanks — sincerely." He was passing some notes at me with his left hand, holding it close to his chest so that they couldn't see from the lounge. The outside wrapping was a brown tenner. It looked like a hundred quid or so.

I shook my head. Just for a moment I wanted to believe we could look at each other without counting the cost.

"Take it for God's sake," he said.

"I'd rather know what this was all about," I said wearily. "Anyway, you paid me for two days in advance. Going to bug me for the rest of my life, wondering what the hell I was involved with here."

He sighed and stared across the tops of the trees. "Funny," he said quietly, "comes a time you'd rather look at a tree than a woman. Never thought it would happen to me. I'm fifty-two, Jim, still haven't found peace of mind. All right, I'll tell you. Simple really. You know I put twenty-five grand or so into Lou's so-called entertainment conglomerate? Going to be a show business tycoon, I thought, no more farting about with dull old furniture. Yeah, big plans, our own recording studio, discover new groups, set up our own label — tomorrow the world. Know what I discovered? That bastard — he's into hardcore porn — smuggles it in from the Continent. Used my capital to take over four or five retail outlets and buy bigger loads of the filthy stuff in Denmark. By the time I twigged I was in as deep as him — at least that's how it would look if we were caught. The bastard used one of my consignments of furniture from Stockholm to bring in a batch — I can't tell you the kind of filth it is, Jim — make you *sick*, animals, children even — no, I couldn't even begin to tell you. So that's it. This hoaxer bastard has found out about me — I can't go to the cops or the whole shooting match comes out and I go down. What do I get — five years?"

The wind was coming across his head the wrong way. His dyed black hair kept standing up on end like the top of a hard-boiled egg. He kept smoothing the flap down on his skull and it kept standing up again.

"Have I got it straight? You invest twenty-five grand with Nicholas to set up an entertainment company? Then you twig he's a porn merchant and he's been using your money to expand that side of it and you're bang in the middle of it? Couldn't you have got out when you first tumbled to it?"

"Maybe. You see, we both went over to Denmark, I was getting together a consignment of kitchen furniture for a cut-price postal offer — you know, the stuff they assemble themselves? He said he wanted to scout around the Danish promoters about our artistes. He told me he'd bought some items for his own house, could I put his crates in with the container? When it got to our warehouse in Luton he showed me what was in the crates. Oh Christ, I didn't know what to do — it was all under my name, my company — "

"Yeah but — "

"I decided to go along with him till I saw a way of getting my cash back out of the company. That's why the open-air festivals looked so good — I'd rip off as much as I could from the gate money and then get out."

"What happened — Nicholas get to it first?"

He frowned. He thought for a moment. Then he shook his head. "No, we had a complete breakdown of where the takings all went, he couldn't have — "

"Listen, that kind of deal, he only has to put in three or four bent gate-men and they'd weed out the take. Did he ever admit outright he deliberately got you involved in the porn smuggling?"

"Well no — we had the shops, he said he thought I would've known it was that kind of business."

"You could've gone to the cops there and then of course."

"I suppose so. Thing was, Jim — well, why lie about it, two weeks later he gave me seven thousand in cash as my share of that load. It's a lot of money, Jim, cash, to make it legitimately you'd have to earn thirty thousand or so before tax."

"You were trapped but the trap had its compensations, eh? The smuggling still going on, is it?"

He rubbed his forehead. "I'm trusting you with my life, Jim — there's twenty thousand quid's worth waiting to be distributed right now."

"Are you saying you'd really like to slide out of the whole deal? Or is all that cash money too sweet to throw away?"

"I'd do anything to get out, if there was a way."

"You got fifteen grand?"

"I could rake it up if I really had to, I mean, if it meant the difference between Simone . . . "

His voice lost interest. He stared out over the park. The wind was getting colder. His hair went up on end. He didn't bother to pat it down. I turned my back on the breeze. Inside the big glass windows I could see vague shadows of people moving about. Beevers was a bit wet about the eyes.

"If you told Nicholas you wanted out — what would happen?"

"I'd lose most of our twenty-five thousand capital. It's not a business with a lot of tangible assets — we've invested in a couple of groups who haven't started earning yet, we paid for the office lease, publicity, office equipment, wages — "

"You put up the lolly, didn't you? You must own the most of it."

"I don't have the know-how to run that kind of agency, Jim — and Lou doesn't have the capital to buy me out. My only hope's to stick close to him and salvage what I can."

"Only if you stick to him you're always going to be ripe for blackmail, aren't you? I mean, do you *really* want out, Mr Beevers?"

"I know Lou, he's a hard bastard

underneath all that smooth crap — getting out wouldn't be so easy."

"You don't think there's a chance he's behind these sick jokes, do you?"

He shook his head emphatically. "Not likely at all, Jim, I'd swear on it. He's not the type."

"You sure?"

"Positive. Take my word for it. I mean, he was in the car with us, wasn't he?"

"The windscreen? Why's that worry you so much in particular? I'd say it was odds-on to be some drunk kid who couldn't get into the game, just chucked a rock at the big cars to show you rich swine — "

"You really think so?"

"Nobody could've known where you were going to make the little fellow park the vehicle, could they? No look, Mr Beevers, there's two things I can do here. Say thanks for the two days' work and the Cup Final ticket and push off. Or help you get out of this hole."

"How could you possibly do it?"

"It doesn't take a Brain of Britain to see a few angles. First off, did you tell Nicholas about these hoaxes and whatnot?"

"No."

"All right then, let's tell him. After all, he's got to be worried, too, hasn't he? He could get the same treatment. Maybe you'll both decide to get shot of the porn game altogether, wriggle out while there's still time. By the way, you know where the stuff is kept?"

"Not in the shops, they're only a means to attract potential customers. There's a lock-up garage in Kensal Green — one of his blokes rents it under a fake name."

"That the only place?"

"No, they move it about until it can be distributed — a lot of it goes up north, Manchester, Liverpool and thereabouts."

"You don't take any part in the actual business of moving it, though?"

"No, I keep thinking the less I know the more chance I'd have in court of saying — well, silly to even hope — "

"All right, let's give Nicholas the full strength of it and see what he says. Just one thing, Mr Beevers — if I'm working for you and you're mixed up in the porn game — well, could be a bit tricky for me, know what I mean?"

He must have heard that tone in people's voices a few times. "Jim, you get me free of all this and I'll pay you — two thousand, sound fair?"

"Very fair. Okay then, let's get hold of Nicholas."

We looked at the big windows. With the reflection of the clouds on glass it was impossible to see the faces. He went inside. I leaned on the balcony. Maybe I was learning about life. Or at least about how to grab some for myself.

I can't say I felt like shouting across the park in triumph. Still, that's what hands are for, isn't it, *grabbing*?

He came back out. "He's gone back to his house with Barbara."

"Chelsea, isn't it? Let's make tracks — sooner this is sorted out the better."

When he told Simone we were going out she wasn't pleased. For a change he acted pretty firm. "We have to see Lou urgently, I won't be long — if anybody rings for me just say I'm out. I'll ask Nathan and Debbie if they'll hang around here till I get back."

"What's wrong?" she said to me.

I winked. "It's a date we got with these two birds we met at Wembley, Liverpool girls, only sixteen, mind, but with a bit of a wash — "

She was too sophisticated to nag at him with a lot of questions. She just refused to speak to him.

★ ★ ★

Godfrey Street is tucked away in the heart of Chelsea, only a few yards from the trendy bustle of the King's Road boutiques but so quiet it could be a private street somewhere round the Mediterranean. The dinky little houses are painted in different colours, cream, white, even bright blue.

We came in from Cale Street, past Sutton Dwellings, five-storey council blocks of the old redbrick sort. There's no Berlin Wall to keep the Dwellings from fraternizing with the yellow doors.

I had to park the Stag farther down. We walked back to a snazzy little house with white walls and window boxes.

It's the doors tell you most about

211

what class of cash lives in a London
street. Down there it was oak or bright
yellows — one even had a glass door
with wrought-iron masking.

"Nice, innit?" I said to Beevers as he
was on the button.

"Oh yes, couldn't get one of them for
much less than fifty thou," he said.

"Be a strong Labour ward then, eh?"

He snorted. Two doors up a young
gent came out wearing a tweed jacket
and a brown trilby hat resting on his
fireman's. "Cheery ho then, me hearties,"
he neighed back to his friends. He got
into an open sports car, one of those
big old jobs with leather straps on the
bonnet. Growl growl, woof woof and off
he shot, to some mess or another.

A small, olive-skinned woman came to
the door. She looked at us a bit stupidly.
"Mr Nicholas?" Beevers said. "Tell him
it's Phil."

"Who is it?" we heard his voice
shouting. The small woman turned
away and shouted something in foreign.
Spanish maybe, I wasn't too clever at
school with English never mind the
difficult ones. Beevers pushed in past

her. "It's me, Phil," he shouted. The little woman went through to the back of the house, leaving us standing there. It didn't have a hallway or a lobby — one minute you were on the pavement, the next you were in the room. Funny looking room, too.

Nicholas came to the head of spiral stairs that went up from the middle of the room into a round hole in the ceiling. He had a big white towel round his middle. His chest was brown and hairy but he had thin legs. Great invention, clothes, wonder who thought them up in the first place? Blokes with skinny legs I expect.

"Something wrong?" he demanded.

"Yes," Beevers said. "I've run into — "

"Help yourself to drinks, I'll be down when I'm decent."

Beevers threw his sheepskin coat on a long, low, purple sofa.

It was a room for impressing people more than living in. There was a varnished pine floor with jazzy rugs. A couple of white eggshell chairs hung by chains from hooks in the ceiling. On the walls were paintings that weren't painted, shapes hammered out of shiny copper.

213

There was a stone hearth with one of those slow-combustion stoves, little glass doors to let you see the glow. There was a hi-fi set with a glass top and big black speakers in the corners, a rack of LPs on a stone ledge, a pile of cassettes beside the LPs. The windows had venetian blinds instead of curtains. Everywhere you looked was some novelty or another, a harpsichord, an antique phone — in one corner was an actual pinball machine, one of the good old sort with painted palm trees and rows of figures and plenty of lights to flash on and off. I went across and tried the handle.

"What do we say?" Beevers muttered urgently.

"Show him the note, tell him the whole story. I used to be pretty good on these machines — I suppose he's got a stock of old pennies to work it."

"For God's sake, Jim! I'm worried sick."

"Just tell him the truth. Have a drink and take it easy."

He looked a bit square in that snazzy room, still in the fawn twill suit he'd worn to Wembley. His shoes were black with laces, very old-fashioned. I hadn't noticed before just how big his plates actually were, size thirteen maybe. A big frightened man with big flat feet. The dyed black hair looked pretty pathetic as well.

Nicholas came down the spiral stairs buttoning the sleeves of a slim-fitting, floral-pattern shirt. His hair was wet and newly combed, dark and sleek as a bullfighter's.

Only he had skinny legs behind the tailoring so I wasn't quite so impressed.

"This was waiting for me at the desk when I got back from the Final," Beevers said, giving him the brown envelope. Nicholas gave me a cold look. He took out the white sheet. Beevers looked at me while he was reading it. I gave him a wink.

"Well well," Nicholas said. He looked at us both. "There's more, is there?"

Beevers started to sit on the purple sofa but it was a bit low and instead he went right over on to his back. Tell the truth I liked him better looking a bit foolish, sort of helped to cover the fact that we only knew each other because of his money.

I leaned on the pinball machine.

"I didn't want to bother you with it, Lou," said Beevers, his face red with embarrassment plus the strain of pulling himself on to an even keel again. "It looks more serious than I thought. About two months ago . . . "

He told it more or less the way he'd told me in the *Three Colts*. Nicholas didn't say a word. He had prominent cheek-bones and tight cheeks. A very *concentrated* man you would say, stylish and precise.

" . . . and then this note turns up so we know what the motive is," Beevers finished up.

"What does he know?" Nicholas said, looking at me.

"Mr Beevers told me about your interests in fine literature," I said.

"Was that wise, Phil?"

Beevers managed to get up from the sofa without much more effort than it would take to move a small tree. He sat on the stone ledge beside the rack of LPs. "I should've phoned Scotland Yard?" he said bitterly. "I can trust Jim — he's the first person I've met recently

216

who actually refuses money."

"You should have consulted me."

"Until this note came I thought I was dealing with Tony Manders."

"This is very bad," Nicholas said. "First of all — "

Barbara came to the top of the stairs. She was wearing an inch of white panties and a bra that might have covered two new pennies. "Am I supposed to sit up here all bloody night?" she said.

"Yes," said Nicholas.

"Piss off," she shouted, "I'm sick of you."

From there I got a smashing view of the pink parts of her feet. Very alluring I dare say. Nicholas took his time about going up the stairs. Beevers and I grimaced at each other. We heard a door closing and some muffled snarling. "Seemed such a polite girl at the football," I said. He mouthed something at me.

"Come again," I said.

"What do I say next?"

"Let me put my oar in."

"Are you sure you know what you're doing?"

"Important thing is — what's he going to do?"

Nicholas came back down the stairs. Not a single black hair out of place. A cool bastard. "No, I don't like this at all," he said, meaning me I presumed.

"Well the point is I've seen Manders and I'm sure he isn't in it," I said. "So that means somebody else has twigged what you're at. You got a choice — you go along with this joker and try to nab him when he collects. Or you quickly give the porn game the elbow. If he knows about Mr Beevers he knows about you as well, Mr Nicholas."

"I could've handled this without bringing in outsiders," Nicholas said. He went across to a glass-fronted bookcase that was actually a cocktail cabinet. He gave Beevers a scotch. I shook my head. He took a thin bottle of white wine and a glass to one of the egg-shaped chairs hanging from the ceiling. It looked as comfortable as a day-trip in a dustbin. He poured some wine and took a careful sip.

It suddenly occurred to me he'd seen a lot of early Dirk Bogarde films. Nothing against Dirk but it isn't a pose you see a lot of these days. Reminds people too much of early Dirk Bogarde films I expect. Or else eyebrows aren't as mobile as they used to be.

"I want to get out of pornography altogether," Beevers said.

"It's not that simple, Phil."

The girl came down the stairs in her long fur coat and leather suit. She went straight to the door and out into the street without saying a dicky bird. Nicholas didn't give her a second glance, not even a first glance for that matter.

"I think I know this situation better than you do, Phil," Nicholas said. "We're in a tricky business, a cash business, we're bound to attract rough customers. Some bright bastard had taken a lot of trouble to set you up. I'm going to have words with Tommy Ableman. I trust him — if only because he has a stake in our operation. Tommy's up in Manchester but I'll give his hotel a ring tonight. I'm willing to bet he can put a name to this anonymous friend of yours. Tommy will know how to handle it."

"You think it's one of our blokes?" Beevers said.

"Maybe. Listen, you are coming tomorrow, aren't you?" He looked at me. "I'm having a little barbecue sort of thing on the roof — providing the weather is kind. I'll have had a chance to speak to Tommy by then. Why don't you come with Phil?"

"Okay," I said. He smiled at Beevers.

"Don't worry, Phil, you can't expect to make our kind of money without some aggro."

"This isn't just some hooligan trying to crash in," Beevers protested. "I don't want Ableman stirring up a lot of trouble."

Nicholas shook his head.

"I'm only guessing but you remember that chap Wordsworth — the one who sold the shops to us in a panic when they were having that last clean-up? He's probably regretting he sold so cheaply now that he sees the market booming again. If it is him I'm sure Tommy will know how to handle it."

"I hope so, Lou."

We left the best of chums. I drove

Beevers to King's Road and then pulled into the kerb.

"I don't imagine he keeps a record of the places they use to store the stuff," I said.

"He does — I'm not supposed to know, of course — I did a little snooping through his desk, he has a file — why?"

"You do want out, don't you?"

"Jim, I've told you — "

"Okay. So this is what we do. You get me the addresses and I'll have it away with the stuff, store it somewhere else. Monday you tell him you're dissolving the partnership. He thinks he's got you by the short and curlies so he'll say — go if you like but your dough stays here with me. Then you say — okay but if you want your filthy books back you'll need to pay me. Screw what you can out of him — fifteen grand? Maybe more? It's like an ace up the sleeve, Mr Beevers."

He blew hard. "Christ, Jim, that sounds very dangerous — "

"All right, pay the man when he phones up. Then start saving up another fifteen grand for the next time he puts the bite on you — they'll let you go in time, Mr Beevers, when you're down to playing the harmonica in the street."

He shivered a bit. "All right — we'll go up to the office now."

"No, I got something else that needs doing. I'll phone you later on tonight. You dig out the addresses, okay? You'll pick up a taxi about here easy enough."

"Oh."

"Don't *worry*, Mr Beevers, I'm on your side."

He got out of the car and lumbered off along the pavement. He looked pretty pathetic among all the sharpies and trendies of the King's Road, just a big fat man without his car and his possessions, no chance to impress people by waving his bundle.

I took the first left back to Cale Street and parked on the corner of Godfrey Street, where I could see Partner Lou's suave little box.

I settled down for a spot of hanging about.

Funny place, Chelsea. Flash, maybe a bit sick behind the cute yellow doors. Like a village that's let daddy's money go to its head.

An hour and a half later this white Jaguar turned in from Cale Street and slid down Godfrey Street looking for a clear space. I had my head well down and my disguise on. Only a flat cloth cap to hide my fair hair.

Out of the Jaguar came two men. One was Danny Aldous, unmistakable round shoulders in a leather jacket.

The one who locked the car was big and bald, with spectacles. He was wearing a dark suit. From that distance I couldn't see his face too well but he didn't look like a Chelsea vicar on the knocker for the fabric fund.

They both stood in front of the house with the white walls and window boxes. Then the door opened and they went inside.

I didn't know what it proved but I was sure it meant something. Maybe if I went to a private detective, a real one, with bugging devices and fancy cameras . . .

I decided to drive somewhere and get something to eat at normal prices.

12

"COH, I'm dying inside I am," groaned my uncle, Cousin Tel. It was a beautiful Sunday morning, only half past eight. We were in his Bedford van headed west on City Road.

"I don't have any hangover," I said, "know why? Not a single fag did I have all last night. That's what does the real damage, smoking."

"Oh yeah — the twelve pints and the bottle of dimple — they're only details, arrey? I thought you said this was all legit — wot's the need for bein' up so bleedin' early?"

"Not so many people about."

"But if we're on *legal* business — "

"The people don't know that, do they? Have a kip, it's a long way to Harlesden."

"When you come to the door last night I thought — how nice. Might ov known you had a *motive*."

I'd kipped down on their sofa for the

night rather than move their three kids about. They had a three-bedroom flat in a high-rise in Hoxton. I'd be lying if I said that was the life I yearned for because it was the life I'd left, by choice, but after the weird doings of the money people a few pints and some Chinese spare-ribs to take home with a bottle of scotch felt like a cool breeze in a hot sock.

I'd phoned Beevers at nine. He gave me two addresses, a lock-up in N.W.10 and a workshop behind a house in W.10. He said the man who lived in the house with the workshop was very old and half-blind, which was why they'd chosen it to store the stuff. I said I'd drop up to Inverson Court about one o'clock.

"So wot is it we gotta do exactly?" Tel asked.

"We effect an entry into a lock-up garage and a workshop and we grab some filthy books and we take 'em to *your* lock-up garage — simple, innit?"

"Wot happens if the people see us an' scream for law?"

"They won't think we're up to anything

dodgy in daylight, will they? All we got to do is act natural — on the other hand, maybe you look like a thief when you're acting natural. Act unnatural — like innocent."

"Do me a favour."

"You got the tools to get into a lock-up garage and a workshop, have you?"

"I dunno, do I? I mean — "

"Last night you said — "

"Oh yeah, last night, twelve pints in me, I'd've been game to crack the Royal Mint, wouldn't I? And wot if I get collared in possession of this bent lirrachewer?"

"I'm working for the bloke who owns half of it."

"So why're we breakin' in?"

"His partner keeps the keys. Get some shut-eye for Christ's sake."

He sat up and checked his eyes in the mirror. They were red and crusted. That seemed to satisfy him. He looked across at me curiously. "Funny sorts you get mixed up wiv in your line, Jim-Jim — issair a livin' innit?"

"How much am I bunging you for this

job you mean? How does a cockle now and a long 'un when I get paid off grab you?"

Cockle means ten pounds — cock and hen, ten. A long 'un is a hundred quid. My uncle didn't need the translation. He thought it sounded like a good deal but he wasn't born yesterday.

"How much are you coppin'?" he asked suspiciously.

"A bit more than that."

"Yeah?"

"What are you up to mainly these days anyway?"

"This and that. Bin doin' a bit wiv country auctions an' that, buyin' gear cheap and floggin' it up here. Nuffink too dodgy — just a bit bent here and there, know wot I mean?"

"I can guess. Give the old lady ten bob for the Rembrandt?"

"Nah, we don't take pianos."

We reached the Harrow Road. There wasn't much traffic about. We passed a bunch of West Indians dressed for church, white hats and stiff suits and kids with bows and Bibles. "Must say, they turn the kids out neat, doaney?"

227

said Tel. "More religious minded than us I expeck."

"Everybody's more religious minded than us. When was you last in a church?"

"Do me a favour."

Farther up the Harrow Road sleepy men in shirt sleeves and slippers were coming out of corner newsagents with the Sunday papers under their arms. The sky was cloudy with bits of blue.

"I always like it this time in the morning," I said, "air's clean, sometimes you could almost think it was the seaside."

"Not in bleedin' Hoxton you couldn't."

"Got your holidays fixed up this year?"

"Yeah, Malta again — well, we did fink of Norf Africa but Sheree don't fancy riskin' the kids wiv all that dodgy food. You goin' anywhere?"

"Dunno."

He twisted round to have a stare at me. "Wot's the scene wiv you anyway, Jim-Jim — niver hear you talkin' about a steady bird or that."

"I only caught the last steady in kip with her bleeding teenage cousin the other night."

"Pity about you an' Jackie reelly."

"Yeah. Still, she's happier now I expect. Got two kids I hear."

"Gonna git hitched again are yer?"

"Miss Right is round the next corner!"

"You always hear about Miss Right, niver about Mrs bleedin' Right."

"Come off it, you're thriving, aren't you? She's a good sort, Sheree, and the kids — don't know how lucky you are."

"I'm always hearin' how lucky I am from single geezers. The joys ov family life — always from blokes who don't have three nippers to keep in noo bloody shoes."

"I think we're getting close. Look out for Furness Road on our right."

We missed it first off and had to come back again. We turned left into the Sunday morning streets of suburban Harlesden, more spades going to church, a bloke stripping a car, three lads setting off on bikes with fishing-rods in canvas bags, two seagulls on the chimney pots.

The lock-up garages were back from the pavement beside some kind of builder's yard and next door to a garden with a wooden wall. I backed the Bedford over the pavement and on to the concrete apron.

We sat there looking at the houses opposite. "All still in kip I expeck," he said. "So wot's the plan?"

"I'll put the hood up and look like I'm working on the engine. You see to the lock. Nobody's going to bother us but if anybody gets busy we just say we forgot the key."

"Let's git on wiv it then."

I had the back of the van about four yards from the battered blue doors. Kids had put *Loft Rule — OK?* on every one of the doors with a white spraycan. Tel disappeared behind the van while I got the bonnet up.

I leaned on my elbows watching the pavement and the houses opposite. Nobody stirred. I hoped they were sleeping off bad hangovers in the semi-detached houses opposite. Tel came round and had a look under the hood.

"There's a lock, it's easy enuff but there's a padlock as well."

"Get it off then — what's the problem?"

"No problem. Gonna be a bit noisy

though, I shall have to rip it off, won't I?"

"I'll sing at the top of me voice, that'll drown it."

Nothing moved in the upstairs windows opposite. I heard the banging then a splintering noise. "Okay," he said. I went round to the back of the van. He pulled one of the doors open and we looked into the darkness.

"You do dog-eye, I'll have a butcher's," I said. "Whatever there is we just bung in the van and scarper, all right?"

"Coh, I feel terrible."

I went to the back wall.

The place was empty.

Not a sausage.

I went back outside and got my head under the bonnet. "Can you put it back the way it was — screw in the plate again maybe?"

"Wot about the gear?"

"None there. See if you can make it look as if we haven't been."

"I'll do my bestest."

Ten minutes later we were shooting along Scrubs Lane along the east side of Wormwood Scrubs. A man was walking

231

his dog and away across the big park we could see the turrets of the prison. It was too early for the football games to have started.

"This one could be trickier," I said, "there's an old man lives in the house — it's a workshop or something at the back. I dunno how near we'll get the van."

"They won't have to look too close to suss somebody was at that padlock back there."

"No sweat, they won't be screaming for law these chaps."

It was a big old house just off St Quintin Avenue at North Pole Gardens. There seemed to be more people on the move.

The house was falling to bits. Where there once had been a wall and a front garden was now just rubbish land. We drove past slowly, seeing the big wooden workshop building behind the house.

"I'll back up the side of the house just like before," I said. "If the old geezer comes out we've been sent to pick up some gear for Fred, right?"

"Who's Fred?"

"I see him as a short man with red cheeks and a weakness for picking his nose. How do you see him?"

"Oh, *that* Fred."

The van bumped over the low kerb. Not so clever that time, I wasn't used to the van and first off I managed to touch the corner of the house. It was a very tight fit between the side wall and the big overgrown hedge. When I got her out on the waste-dump that used to be the back lawn, we sat for a few moments to see if anybody was stirring in the house.

"Shame them places goin' to ruin," said Tel.

"You going to sit there all day being sentimental?"

Getting into the workshop was a trickier proposition.

"Gonna have to screw off the padlock plate," Tel said, "could take time."

"What about the lock?"

"No problem to an expert."

"If you give me one more chance, Your Honour, I swear I'll go straight. Get going then for Christ's sake."

I got on the other side of the van so

that I could lean under the hood and watch the back of the house. The sun was making it quite warm. Half the windows in the house didn't have curtains.

A cat came slinking across the bricks and rubbish. Little sparrows dived in and out of a dead bush drowning in green creeper. Just for a moment it felt like a spring day in the countryside.

The old man came out of the house by the side door!

Shit!

He started to walk up the side of the house. He was carrying something. I made a hissing noise to tell Tel but I didn't think he heard. The old fellow came out into the sunshine. He was wearing a new-looking brown jacket with a thin scarf round his neck.

He put his hand over his eyes and looked all round.

When he spoke I was sure he was talking to me.

We couldn't have been more than fifteen yards apart.

"Come on then, breakfast is ready," was what he said.

Half-mad as well was he?

The cat had its tail straight up in the air as it shot across the rubbish and bent its spine round his leg.

"You been out all night again," he said.

Then he turned and went slowly back into the shadow of the house, his hand touching the wall, the cat jinking about his legs and twisting its head against his trousers.

Then Tel said something and I went round the back of the van.

"You watch," I said. "Don't make any noise."

"Give us one of those naughty books to pass the time."

The workshop was big enough to hold two or three cars. It had a bench with vices and various tools hanging on nails. The concrete floor was black with dirt and oil. All along the walls were old jerricans and oilcans and bits and pieces of metal.

At the back there were two wooden crates!

As I went up to them I was looking round for a tyre-lever or something to force them open but it wasn't necessary.

Soon as I lifted the first lid off I saw I'd struck gold. It was a magazine called *Thrill*, a red cover with a picture of a ferocious woman's face and a big headline — *Tyrants Of The Bedchamber*! The way it was lying on top it had obviously been taken out of a square brown parcel. The cover was creased, the sample for browsing I supposed.

I had a look in the second crate. On the top of its brown paper parcel was another magazine, *Thrust*. The photo showed a woman in Nazi gear holding a whip to her cheek. *I Was A Lust Slave of The Wehrmacht Nympho Squad* was the main attraction.

I pulled up the brown parcel. There was another parcel underneath. They didn't have any labels. The crates were unmarked.

I went outside and hissed for Tel. We had a look at the house and went inside. "There you go," I said, handing him the two magazines, "don't let it corrupt your innocent mind. Twenty grand in this little lot — must be sizzling stuff."

Tel frowned. "Give us a look." He thumbed through the one about the Nazi lady. "I've read it," he said.

"Do what?"

"Yeah, it's about this Yank pilot in the war, he comes down and the kraut home guard nabs him — only they're all wimmin. Twenty grand's worth did you say?"

"Where did you read it?"

"My mate Slippery gits 'em all the time. You sure this is the right gear?"

I dived into the crate and ripped off brown paper. I pulled that parcel out and then the next.

Five minutes later we'd been through every brown paper parcel in the two crates. I wiped my face with my sleeve.

"You're right," I said, "this is ordinary tit'n'bum stuff. Now why the hell . . ."

"Come on, Steve Austin, wot we do now then?"

"Bung these parcels back upside down, maybe they won't spot we've been at them. Then we get the hell out of it."

It took Tel about ten minutes to screw the padlock plate back on. He said he would drive this time, the morning's exercise having cured his head.

As we rolled up the side of the house

the side door was open. Maybe the old fellow heard us but if he did we were long gone before he made it to the pathway.

"Did we achieve anythin' notable or what?" Tel asked as we got on to Westway and headed back east.

"I dunno. This bloke puts twenty-five grand into a business. An entertainment agency sort of. Next thing he twigs his partner is deep into porn smuggling. He's in a spot — if the law tumbles who's going to believe he didn't know anything? He gets seven grand as his share of one batch so he isn't all that bothered — seven grand cash money, readies, no tax. Next thing some joker starts playing hoaxes on him only they begin to get more menacing until yesterday he gets a note saying if he don't come up with fifteen grand they're going to give his wife the treatment. They say they know he's into the porn caper so he isn't likely to want the Old Bill crawling over his private affairs. But . . . "

"Go on, I'm gittin' excited, wot happens next?"

"Thing is, I've a notion his partner might be the anonymous hoaxer. So I say I'll grab the naughty books and stash them somewhere else. That way he can wriggle out from the partnership without losing all his dough — he can flog the gear back to the partner. Only we've just discovered the filthy books aren't all that filthy — ordinary family reading by today's standards. That's the puzzle. He told me they showed him one of these magazines that almost made him heave."

"Yeah? Wot was it like? Real hot, was it? Coh — "

"Do shut up. I got to think."

"Think out loud then, I'm dead curious to hear how it ends. Better' Cannon it is, I mean on that one they always show you who dunnit first, like Colombo, not a real mystery at all — "

"For Christ's sake, Tel! What's that out there? A motorway, right? Motor cars. The sun shining on the rooftops of North bleeding Kensington. This isn't the bleeding telly, this is you and me in real life, dumbo. I get two grand coming my way if I can sort this one out — "

"Two grand? You rotten berk! An' I'm gittin' cigarette money? Cor, pullin' a stroke on your own flesh an' blood!"

"Did I say two grand? Slip of the tongue. Don't worry, you'll get your tenner — "

"And a hundred."

"That's only if I can sort this lot out."

"Seems simple enuff to me, Jim-Jim."

"Oh yeah? Watching Colombo has made you the new Sherlock, has it?"

"All I can see is money, Jim-Jim. Bloke puts in twenty-five grand, gets seven back. If he has a mind to complain he's told he's mixed up in dirty lirrachewer. Next fing it's freatenin' his missus — fifteen grand or she gets hurt. If he has a mind to complain — same story, he'll get weighed off for smugglin' dirty lirrachewer. So wot do they end up wiv? His first twenty-five grand plus this next fifteen grand? Minus the seven grand they bung him as sweetenin' money. He's gettin' cleaned out, innee? Like the old corner game innit, set the mug up to buy somefink bent and then have it away wiv his readies — he can't scream for law cos how he gonna explain to the Old Bill he was buyin' bent gear?"

240

I could hardly bear to speak for two minutes.

I said eventually, in my quietest voice, "All they needed was a couple of ripe magazines to kid him on. Hell's bloody teeth . . . "

"You can't win 'em all, Jim-Jim," he said.

He was smirking all over his fat face.

★ ★ ★

It was about one when I got back to Regent's Park. The sun was shining and all the smart people were walking their dogs. Some of them were even walking their kids. I slid the Stag down into the gloomy basement.

Pat of the narrow shoulders was on duty at the desk. "You got the job I hear," he said as I went past, "hope it goes all right for you."

"Yeah, thanks."

When I got out on the seventh floor these two mysterious nuns were waiting to go down. Only they weren't nuns, they were Arabs in white desert gear. They didn't smile and I didn't ask how

241

many Miss Rights they had between them. From the back they still could've been nuns.

Beevers was wearing a blazer, white trousers, silk cravat and dark blue shirt.

"You should've told me it was fancy dress," I said.

"Oh there you are, Jim, come in." He fingered me to bend an ear. "Simone and I are having the most awful row," he whispered.

"You told her about the note?" I whispered back.

He frowned and shook his head. "No — that's not what it's about — she wants to take Jason to Lou's place but I'm not having that — "

Honest to God. I got hold of his arm and made him come out into the corridor. He was twice as wide as me but he was as hard to move as a bucket full of flies.

"You're having a row about the bleeding dog?" I could have hit him. He came over apologetic very quickly.

"It's my nerves, Jim, don't think I'm not taking this seriously — I just don't seem able to — "

"Yeah yeah. Good job nothing serious ever happened to you, like the birds pecking off your bottle tops. We're going in there and you're going to tell her the lot, right?"

"Do we have to? I mean — "

"If anything did happen to her how would we look? Threats being made against her and we kept it quiet?"

He looked properly ashamed. "You're right, Jim."

"Okay then, let's tell her."

He patted his pockets. Honest to God. No key!

13

WHEN she finally opened the door she was wearing big dark shades — very menacing. An optician once told me the sun is never strong enough in this country to hurt the eyes.

Certainly not inside the house.

"The wind blew the door shut," I said, "can we come in?"

She walked away and slammed the bedroom door. I went into the lounge so that he could do his pleading in private.

In the sunshine the balcony view was something else again. Funny how you only see bricks and dirt when you're down there. From up high London looked like a suburb of Epping Forest. I sat on a white iron chair. I got my fags. There was enough of a breeze to blow out the match before I got lit up.

They came out of the french doors, her in front. She was wearing a dark blouse with a tight white skirt, bare legs and white sandals with platform soles. Soon as he saw me with a fag in my mouth he whisked out his gas lighter and shoved a three-inch flame in my face.

I took the fag out of my mouth and flicked it over the balcony. "Killing fifty thousand people a year supposed to be," I said. I threw the rest of the packet on the white table. "Funny that, I always thought it'd be difficult to give 'em up."

He brought the brown envelope out of his hip pocket and handed it to her. He put his hands on the balcony and looked out over the park. She sat down opposite me and read the note, shoving the dark glasses up on top of her white-gold hair.

When she looked up at me I said, "It was handed in at the desk last night. That's why we went to see Lou Nicholas. Just a chance he knew who's the joker behind this malarkey."

She looked up at him. "What does it mean — we know what business you're in and why you can't go to the police?"

Whatever he said went out into the big

blue sky. "Don't mumble," she snapped.

"Lou smuggles pornography into the country," he said, speaking slowly, forgetting to keep his shoulders back and his belly in. "It wasn't my idea, I didn't even know about it until it was too late. Jim — know what I realized when I went through his file last night? My initials are typed on the memo sheets with the addresses. Anybody looking at them is going to assume I'm the one."

"Yeah, it's a racing cert that flies skid when they land on Lou Nicholas."

We looked at each other. A jumbo jet turned towards Heathrow high above our heads.

"I could do with a drink," he said. "Simone? Jim?"

She shook her head. "If you had a beer," I said.

"I've got the best Danish lager there is in the fridge," he said. Sounded quite indignant, too.

When she and I were alone I put my hands behind my head and stretched. "I got to hand it to you, taking this very well considering, aren't you?"

"One nervous nellie is enough in any

family. What do you suggest we do now?"

"Depends, dunnit?"

"Do you think you could give that act a rest?"

"I told you, the act is when I'm trying to speak grammar."

She pulled the glasses down. Jason strolled out on to the balcony and put his chin on her lap. She gave him a pat and he lay down in a patch of sunlight.

"Dog's life, innit?" I said. "Much does he cost a week in meat and that?"

"For God's sake — "

"No, I'm interested. Five quid?"

"He gets a proper diet — a dog like that would starve to death on tinned food."

"*More* than five? He'll be paying income tax soon I reckon."

Beevers came out with a tray, a dumpy bottle and a tall glass for me, a big scotch with ice in a crystal glass for him. Plus a little plate of peanuts. Honest to God. He sat down. He looked about as relaxed as six men with one lifebelt. I felt like asking him if he ever got any real enjoyment out of life but it was the psychiatrist he paid for the philosophical chit-chat.

"Well, I got some news for you," I said. "I cannot tell a lie, I was thinking of not telling you this until after you paid me the two grand we agreed on — "

"Now, Jim!"

"Yeah yeah, I know, you wouldn't stoop so low as to chisel me out of a lousy two grand — listen, Mr Beevers, it's the oldest law in nature, when the money comes up the stairs the principles dive out the window. Nice drop of lager this."

"I wish we could hear this news," she snapped.

"I had a look in the two places you gave me addresses for — one was bare, the other had a coupla crates of tame stuff you can buy in sweetshops these days."

"But the stuff he's bringing in is filth!"

"The one he showed you maybe — look through the lot, did you?"

"Well no — but I saw him tearing the parcel open — "

"Yeah?"

"You mean — no, he wouldn't have

248

gone to all that trouble — "

"People are breaking their backs to drag down thirty quid a week, Mr Beevers — you think making up a few parcels is too much trouble for forty grand?"

"Forty grand? What do you mean?"

"Who does the books in your company?"

"The book-keeper — and every month the accountant checks the book-keeper's figures."

"Whose accountant?"

"Well — Lou's actually."

"Who hired the book-keeper?"

"Ehm, well — Lou did."

"Thought so. Mind you, he could be storing the real stuff in some other place. We got to make sure about that."

"I told you he was a snake," she snapped at Beevers. Poor Mr B, he'd just been kissed by the electric hammer.

"You really mean it isn't hardcore porn?" he said.

"I took a friend. Bedtime reading in the vicarage he says. By the way, who's a big bloke with a bald head and specs? Travels with that Danny Aldous who was here yesterday."

"That could be Ableman, he's the chap

who actually runs the shops."

"I went back last night and watched Lou's house. He must've been on the blower as soon as we pushed off — Ableman and Aldous showed about an hour later. Only he told us Ableman was in Manchester, didn't he?"

"He bloody did, too!"

"Mutual trust is a wonderful thing. Didn't you find out anything about Nicholas before you casually bunged twenty-five grand in his bin?"

She snorted. He sagged even more. I held the cold glass against my cheek. "I thought I did," he said. "He's very impressive, full of ideas — my own accountant thought it was all fairly reasonable. Of course, it's a business that deals with intangible assets."

"You're a fool," she said, "you didn't care about the assets, you saw him with that black whore and your eyes were popping out of your head. My money, too!"

"It was not your money — not all of it anyway."

She turned the dark glasses on me. "Do you really think Nicholas has been doing all these awful things?"

"Makes sense, doesn't it? He knows your husband can't go to the cops, he knows the set-up here — your husband keeps a spare key in the office — plus the fact that the filthy gear is quite clean, really. I wouldn't fancy my Mum reading it but it wouldn't get you in the dock."

"What do we do now?" he said.

"You're *feeble*," she snapped. To me she said, "What would you advise?"

"When in doubt have it out. Why don't we all go to his rooftop rave-up and just tell him I've twigged to his little caper? If he has any of the real valuable filth tucked away somewhere he can take us to it and prove he's on the level. If not — get your lawyers on to him, grab what you can from the business."

"Oh no — we can't come straight out and accuse him just like that."

"That's exactly what we are going to do," she said. She got up.

Beevers rubbed his forehead. "For God's sake, let's think about it — you don't know Lou as well as I do. He can be very nasty — and he has Ableman."

"I think you'll find for two grand I

can stretch a point and be quite nasty myself," I said, trying to be a bit modest. "Nice drop of lager this."

"I can get you a few crates of it," he said.

Good old Beevers. The roof was falling in but prestige still mattered most.

"Jason!" she called.

"Don't bring the dog for goodness' sake — "

"He hates being stuck in his room on a day like this."

"I'd leave him at home," I said.

"Why — don't you like him?"

"I keep waiting for him to throw me sticks to fetch. Know what I mean?"

"I'll phone for a cab," he said.

"Don't bother, we'll go in my car," I said.

"If we go by cab we can have a few drinks without worrying about the police."

I had to shake my head. "Mr Beevers, you think it's going to be a jolly rave-up?"

We went in my car.

We didn't take the hound.

In the car going to Chelsea he began to lose his bottle. "You can't really just go up and accuse Lou to his face — "

"We'll accuse him to his shoulder-blades then. Either way you're dealing with hooks here, Mr Beevers — if he ain't conning you he's putting you in line for five years away. Porridge and that. *Prison*, Mr Beevers, that's what's looming over you. Last big-scale porn merchant I read about got three years *and* fined ten grand. Plus they confiscated the naughty merchandise. You can bet your name is on every cargo manifest and loading sheet connected with it."

"Oh God."

"Just take it easy. Behave like it was a normal party. I'll get Nicholas on his tod and say I've been doing a bit of scouting around on my own account — I'll give him the opening to offer me a bung. You know, come to an accommodation. Straighten me. Square me — "

"Oh — you mean bribe you to keep you quiet?"

"I wish I knew words like that."

"Very amusing," she said. "Will you take the bribe?"

I gave her an evil grin. She was in front with me. He was filling up the back. "I can't be bought, Mrs Beevers. Except with money."

★ ★ ★

It was a dazzling afternoon and trendy little Godfrey Street was looking very dinky in the sun. Being that class of neighbourhood it wasn't exactly crammed with kids kicking cans. No men in vests stripping rusty motors. No wives in bare legs and slippers scratching their elbows over a bit of gossip. No pigeons picking cold bits from Colonel Sanders's boxes. No six Irishmen swaying together on the corner trying to remember what people did after the boozers closed.

Beevers said from the back seat, "I wouldn't mind having a house here, darling."

"Too chi-chi," she snapped. I parked three or four houses farther on and switched off.

"Bit dead, innit?" I said.

"They'll all be away for the weekend at their country cottages," he explained.

"Yeah? They pay sixty grand to live in a sproncy little street like this and then they rush off to the country? Must be hard to remember where their clothes are."

"You're jealous of people with money," she said, sounding as if she'd just won a guessing game.

"Not the people, just the money. What does it actually feel like to have pots of it, I often wonder. I mean *feel* — know what I mean?"

"Nervous," he said. "I'll tell you one thing, Jim — the real rich spend it quickly. Rats can hear the rustle of pound notes ten miles off."

She snorted. "Poor Philip," she said sarcastically, "he wants to be loved by the rats."

"Shut up, Simone." He put his hand on my shoulder. "Whatever Lou is I don't really know — but Ableman is a real hard case. Watch out for him, Jim."

"I read it in a book — you know that if you stand your ground a gorilla will back away? So if you see a Zulu with teeth marks on his arse you know he's a coward."

"Are we going in or not?" she demanded.

We crossed the quiet street. The foreign woman let us in. She pointed up the spiral stairs.

It was all happening up on the roof. The patio they called it, enough room for twenty people or so among the plants in pots and the white wrought-iron chairs.

The beautiful people mostly, smooth and shiny and seductive. The women were pretty alluring as well.

The patio opened off a snazzy living-room on the first floor. I think somebody called it a drawing-room. The downstairs was all modern, apart from the old-fashioned pinball machine, but up here was the class gear, a shiny black desk with pink china panels, an old wind-up gramophone with a big horn, a globe of the world, prints of old London on the walls, a three-piece leather suite studded with brass buttons.

To get outside we had to pass between two women standing in the french windows. One was a stout party in a floor-length black tent with beads and a red bandanna across her forehead, the other was a strapping blonde athlete sort in a sleeveless summer pinafore. She was about eight months pregnant. She had a glass of wine in one hand and a fag in the other.

"I keep telling her the whole thing is too banal," the fat one was saying, "she will insist on dragging him *everywhere*, such a common lout with his shirt open to his bellybutton — and that gold chain! — I'm even beginning to feel sorry for Justin."

"There you are, Phil — hello Simone darling," Nicholas called from the crowd outside in the sunshine.

"Justin is *weak*," the pregnant one said as it was my turn to pass through. She blew smoke up into the fresh air.

"'Scuse me, ladies," I said.

The fat one in the black drapery gave me an instant smile. She had thick hair, darkish red, probably about forty.

"Are you one of Lou's crimimal friends," she said, quite loudly, too.

"Me?" I was shocked. "Do me a

favour — I'm studying the violin."

The pregnant one sniffed. I gave her a frown. "When I was a surgeon I used to tell 'em that fags is very bad for the unborn child."

"How very droll," she said icily. "You — a surgeon?"

"Well I never actually had a licence or that."

The sun hit my face as I stepped on to the open roof. It had trellis-work round three sides with green creepers to give some privacy from the other patios and roof gardens. It was like walking into the middle of a TV commercial, maybe that one for gin where they're all young and lovely and rich and nobody gets pissed although they're sloshing back enough mother's ruin to frighten a fish-porter.

"There's only one place I'd like to see a Communist," a small man was saying as I passed, "up against a wall."

In one corner, in the shade of the creepers, Lou Nicholas was pouring from a bottle wrapped in a white towel. He was wearing a white tennis shirt and white trousers.

"I hate introductions," he drawled, "if

you see anything you'd like to converse with you just push in. The nosh is over there — better grab some before it vanishes."

Simone said she wasn't hungry. Beevers dived into the little crowd. A fancy-looking specimen with cropped brown hair turned to give us the once-over. "Ah Seemone!" he yelped, raising his arms. He was fairly tall in a black silk shirt and dark trousers with a silver belt. He let his wrists droop over her shoulders and kissed her forehead and then leaned back to admire her. "The most bewteefool woomen een Lon-don!"

He got his right arm round her shoulders and turned her towards the crowd he was with. Among them was Barbara the black girl singer. Most of the men were in check shirts, chokers, cavalry twills.

Not all of them though. In the other corner I saw that same bald head and glasses. Tommy Ableman. Beside him was the round-shouldered Danny Aldous. They were making merry with some nice-looking young people, especially a short girl with freckly brown shoulders sticking out of a yellow blouse.

Just for a moment Nicholas and I were alone behind all the backs.

"He designs cushions," he said, meaning the foreign geezer who'd grabbed Simone, "probably not your type."

"Depends on the cushions I always say." He gave me the lazy, superior smile. I didn't fool him with my little act, oh no. "Any chance you and me could have a quiet chat?" I said.

He cocked an eyebrow. "New developments?"

"Yeah, could be."

Beevers came back with two paper plates. On mine was a hunk of french bread, a square of well done steak, a dab of french mustard, a pat of butter and a knife and fork wrapped in a paper serviette. I put my glass on the wooden table and got to work on the steak.

"Won't be a minute," Nicholas said. He got a new bottle from a metal bucket under the table. He wrapped it in the white towel and worked the cork off with his thumbs.

"The towel is merely to hide the label,"

he said and went off leaving Beevers and me in our shady little corner under the trellis-work. "When are you going to speak to him?" Beevers muttered, sounding very worried, although that could have been caused by the wodge of steak and bread his words had to fight through.

"Soon," I said, looking round the people. "Pretty suave, eh? Never guess out in the street it was all happening up here." Nobody paid us any attention. "Just remember — I haven't told you what I found this morning — all right? You don't know nothing."

He frowned. Nicholas came back and put the empty under the table. He looked pretty fit. Simone was lost by then in the crowd. I used the rest of my champagne to swill down the last of the steak and bread. "Very nice," I said, "best thing for cleaning your teeth there is, drop of steak."

"Ah — there's somebody I must say hullo to," Nicholas said, lifting his hand to wave at some new arrivals. "Tamara!" In a lower voice he murmured, "Where does one gather all these bores?"

Beevers and I watched him doing the kisses and dahlings routine. "I'm going to say to him it's possible Ableman is chiselling the pair of you," I said. "We'll see how he reacts to that."

"I'm frightened, Jim —"

"I should go over there and make sure the cushion-designer isn't offering to show your missus how the stuffing's done. Don't *worry* so, Mr Beevers, the gorilla always backs down first."

I let my tongue slide round my steak-polished railings. The fat woman with the bandanna came across. "My name's Olivia Gillespie, I'm in publishing," she said. "And you?"

"My name's Jim, I'm in pub-crawling."

"What about your violin-playing?"

"I gave it up since I saw you last, didn't have long enough melodies for it, did I?"

She nodded seriously. We were both witty sorts, wasn't it nice?

"The melodies weren't long enough for you?" she said. "I see."

"No, my melodies." I held up my hands. "My melody lingers — fingers."

"Oh I see now — colourful cockney

rhyming slang! Is it normal usage where you come from?"

"No, I'm taking it at GLC night-classes."

"I see you've met Olivia," Nicholas said. "If you'll excuse us for a minute, Olivia — Jim, shall we go inside?"

"Like that with you two is it?" she said, making a funny face.

I followed him through the little chattering circles into the drawing-room. There were a couple of people standing in there, including the pregnant blonde. He nodded for me to come down the spiral stairs to the ground floor.

He had a quick look back up the stairs to make sure nobody was earwigging. "I'm glad of this chance to have a word with you," he said, "like a drink?"

"No thanks." I wandered over to the pinball machine. Painted palm trees and electric mushrooms. "I see your friend Ableman got back from Manchester then," I said.

"I'll introduce you later — what did you want to tell me?"

"You know the score between Beevers and me? He thought these sick jokes were due to his ex-driver, Manders, until that note came. Panicky sort of bloke — you find that?"

He sat on one of the bottom stairs. Didn't bother to wipe it clean and didn't bother to pull up his trouser legs. Sign of real money that, I've always read.

"Are we discussing Phil's nervous temperament?"

"Dunno. You know he's paying me two grand if I sort this lot out for him? I'd better tell you that so you know my angle."

"Your price you mean?"

"Yeah, could be. Anyway, after he tells me about this porn business I reckoned there was a fair chance you could be behind the anonymous caper."

"Me?" He patted his neck and blinked. "You're saying you thought I sent him that note? I want to get this very clear."

"Yeah — maybe you, maybe one of your blokes. It's somebody who knows a lot about Beevers and also about the porn — why shouldn't it be you? After all, you're already in one type of villainy, aren't you?"

"Do go on."

"Anyway, I says to Beevers after we left you last night, why don't you tell me where the gear is being stored and I'll nip round there and shift it. Then if it is you who's putting the bite on him he's got a card up his sleeve, know what I mean?"

"He doesn't know where it's kept. I'm bloody sorry he ever got to know anything at all."

"That lock-up in Harlesden and the workshop in St Quintin Avenue — that's the two places he told me about anyway."

He started to swear and then shut his mouth on it. I gave the pinball bolt a pull and tried the table for possible tilting. It was a bit shaky. "Suppose you need old pennies for this," I said.

"What did you do then?" His voice was a lot chillier.

"I went to these two places this morning. No porn there I could see, was there? Just a coupla crates of tame stuff you can get from the public library these days. Mr Beevers told me you got twenty grand's worth stashed away — but not in those two places you haven't. Thing is, Mr Nicholas, are you conning him or is somebody else conning you both?"

He tried to stare me to death. I folded my arms and leaned against the pinball machine.

"You are saying that you broke into two locked premises? I want to get this clear — "

"I was acting on behalf of Mr Beevers and he's part owner, right? Still, if you want to scream for law go ahead. No? Thought not. So do I tell Mr Beevers there's no filthy literature or what?"

He perked up at that. "You haven't told him yet?"

"He's been under a lot of strain lately. I thought maybe you and me could sort it out between us. Is there any real stuff tucked away somewhere?"

He took a deep breath. "This is a genuine shock to me. You do realize I'm only the paymaster — I never have any physical contact with the stuff? Ableman does all that."

"Maybe he's got another place to store it."

He shook his head. Then he frowned. It was a good act. "Unless — you are quite positive there was nothing worth twenty thousand in those two sheds?"

"No way."

"Look, you know practically everything about this affair — can I tell you something else in the very strictest confidence?"

"Not really."

As I say, nobody listens these days.

"Ableman is a genuine crook, I knew that from the start. He came to me with this proposition to take over four porn shops, a man called Wordsworth was selling quickly because of the big clean-up but Ableman said we could still clear about a hundred a week from each outlet with soft porn — and no problems with the law. I'd put up the capital and Ableman would run the business — he'd been in it before he said, he knew all the angles. He didn't say a word to me but as soon as we had the shops he brought in a load of the utmost degrading filth from Hamburg. He did it to me originally — the shops were in my name, any prosecution would be against me. But the money was good. Then Phil came along wanting to be a show biz tycoon, the usual motivation, when do we audition the starlets sort of thing. Ableman said we could use his capital to buy the stuff in bigger quantities — plus his furniture containers gave us a new way of smuggling it in."

"What's the state of play now then?"

"I gave Ableman five thousand in cash about three weeks ago and he went over to Hamburg and Copenhagen. As far as I knew the load was brought over by a Dutch lorry-driver and we've been waiting to sell it up north."

"That's why Ableman was up in Manchester yesterday, was it? Maybe he's sold the stuff without telling you. Did you speak to him about that note Mr Beevers got?"

He stood up. He had a quick look up the spiral stairs to make sure nobody was listening. He went across to the cupboard with the drinks. "No, I haven't had a chance yet. I called his hotel last night but he'd booked out they said. Would you like a drink?"

"Thanks, I'm all right. So what's it all add up to? Ableman had five grand off you in readies and he told you the stuff he bought with it was stashed away in the lock-up or the workshop. It isn't there so either he's flogged it without telling you or there never was any stuff. In that case what's he planning to do when you ask where the profits are?"

Nicholas drank the way he did everything else, neatly, smooth movements, no energy wasted. He went across the room and put the drink on top of a cute little piano — the old kind, a harpsichord sort of thing.

"There's only one way out of this," he announced. "I'm going to have to think up some excuse to see the stuff. He either has to tell me where it really is or admit that he just pocketed the five thousand. By the way, how did Phil get to know about the lock-up and the workshop?"

"He goes through your desk at night. I don't think he actually trusts you a hundred per cent. Funny, innit?"

A woman's voice came down the stairs. "Are you hiding from us, Lou?"

"Be with you in two shakes," he shouted. He listened for a moment. Then he gave me a pained sort of grimace. "I do a bit of boxing, just to keep in trim — I must say Tommy

Ableman would not be my first choice of a sparring partner. Could be very, very rough."

"Tough nut is he?"

"He told me he killed a chap in his younger days. He's done time in Dartmoor."

"Yeah, sounds very frightening. You think he could be the one doing all these nasty things to Mr and Mrs Beevers?"

"It's highly possible, isn't it? My God, I'm beginning to know what it must feel like to walk across a minefield. Still, what must be done must be done."

I followed him up the spiral stairs.

He was a first-class fanny merchant, I had to give him that. If I hadn't seen Ableman and Aldous arriving the night before I might easily have believed all that spiel.

The interesting thing would be what Ableman decided to do when he heard the good news.

We went through the drawing-room and out into the sunshine. The beautiful people were getting a bit noisier. I slid through them to where Beevers was standing with my witty friend Olivia.

They looked about the right age for each other. Maybe a wife like her would have given him a chance to wear slippers and flop down in front of the telly of an evening.

"It's the backstreet surgeon," she said.

His eyes asked the anxious question.

"Lou's going to ask him about that other matter," I said, looking across to where the inky black head was close to the shiny bald head. I got myself a glass of champagne.

"You're not a surgeon," Olivia said, giving my arm a sly push, "your friend has just told me — you're a private detective."

"He's a bigger liar than I am," I sneered. "Know what his game is — he steals cats for the cheap fur trade. King of the moggy mob, that's him. I hold the sack while he coaxes them to their doom. Horrible, innit?"

She laughed. A big jolly woman. Educated, too. She even managed to make Beevers smile.

Then we both saw Nicholas and Ableman pushing through the people into the darkness of the drawing-room.

Turning my face away from her I muttered, "They'll be back in a minute with whatever yarn they can cook up. He's definitely conning you."

That wiped out his smile.

They came back in about ten minutes, both of them beaming at all the nice people. They looked very confident.

14

WE went on joking with this Olivia lady. Far as I could see Nicholas and Ableman were simply circulating, having a laugh here and there.

Then Ableman came towards us, the black chick Barbara in tow. He was that beefy sort you see a lot of at the football and the fights, a big pink face and a chest that's only just beginning to slip below the belt. A cheery chap.

"Hello there, Mr Beevers," he said, "you know Barbara, donchyer? And you'll be Mr Hazell Lou's told me about? Glad to know yer." He slapped his hands together. The spectacles had no rims. With the shiny bald head and the pink face they gave him a kind of scoutmaster look. Or a bishop, maybe. He had a nice blue suit and a white shirt with a silk tie in a small hard knot. One of the old school you would've said, seen a bit of service in the army, done a bit of rough-housing on the cobbles, no stranger to a bit of ducking and diving but basically one of the chaps.

He slapped his hands again. "Well then, where's the bubbly?" He turned his head. "'Ere, Lou," he bawled, "we're all a bit parched here."

"Help yourself, Tommy, it's under the table," Nicholas shouted back. He was in the same group as Simone and the Eytie cushion-artist.

Ableman bent his broad back and came up with a bottle of champagne. He had big hands, well-scrubbed and manicured but no strangers to hard graft. He gave us all a wink as the cork popped out and the little wisps of vapour escaped.

"Go on, fill yer boots," he said loudly, sloshing into our glasses. I held mine away. "Wot's wrong with you then, squire?" he said jovially. "Give us yer goblet, can't do better'n drop ov bubbly, can yer?"

"I'm all right," I said.

He insisted on trying to grab my glass to fill it up and I wouldn't have any. In trying to give me some he managed to splash my trousers. I said it didn't matter but he came over all apologetic and got out a hankie and tried to wipe at the stain.

He was a big fellow and a bit clumsy. Anybody watching would've spotted him for being just a bit gone on champagne. Trying to wipe my trousers he managed to bang Olivia with his shoulder. She had to grab hold of Beevers to steady herself.

I reached down and got a grip of Ableman's arm. It wasn't soft.

"That's all right," I said, "I'll clean it later." He tried to shrug my hand off but I kept hold until he stood up.

"Sorry about that," he grinned.

His next move made the rest seem quite delicate. He shouted something to Nicholas about getting the music going and then slung his arms round Barbara's neck, still holding his glass in his right hand.

All the champagne that had been in the glass hit me about the chin.

"Sorry about that, mate," he said, laughing and pointing at the drips on my chest, "still, if you won't drink it you

275

can smell it." To Barbara he said, just as loudly, "I hate them creepin' Jesuses puttin' the mockers on the party spirit, know what I mean?"

I ran my palm over my jacket and sweater. Pretty obvious the idea was to rile me into a fight. He hadn't been as drunk as this ten minutes ago. The clever thing would be for me to get the hell out of there.

Only the clever thing isn't always possible, is it?

Beevers saw I was going to speak. He looked terrified and tried to hold my arm.

"Clumsy sort of bastard, ain't you?" I said to Ableman. He took his time about turning his big shiny head to look at me through his rimless glasses.

"Didn't I say sorry?" he said calmly. "An' don't use rude language fronta the ladies."

"Yeah? You an expert on good manners are you, Curly?"

"Do what?" he said quietly.

Faces began to turn. The vibration did a fast ripple across the patio. Voices tapered off.

276

"What's your next trick?" I said. "If you'd any brains you'd be dangerous."

"You makin' some comment about my brains?" he growled.

"Yeah — you tried the lost luggage department?"

"Let's cool it," said Beevers nervously.

"Shut up, Fatso," Ableman snapped. He stretched out his arm and gave my chest a shove with the flat of his hand. "I think you an' me's goin' outside for a bit," he said, "all these people heard you insultin' me."

"We are outside, Curly."

Olivia tried to get between us. "This man was only upset because you spilled — "

He pushed her away. She stumbled against Beevers. "I'm gonna waste you, pal," he growled, "out in the street suit yer?"

"Soon as you like, Curly."

He turned and headed for the door. No sign of being drunk now. "What's wrong?" Nicholas asked as I passed him.

"Your plan's working so far," I snapped at him.

It wasn't exactly subtle but that's the

difference with villains, given the option they prefer the simple short-cut. To anybody watching it was an ordinary flare-up, liable to happen any time when men are drinking.

Only I was down for a hammering that would scare me off for keeps. And what they did to me would also put the frighteners on Beevers.

I was stepping into the drawing-room when I felt somebody at my back. It was Danny Aldous.

"Where are you going?" I said.

He grinned. "I'll hold the jackets and time the rounds," he said.

"You stay here," I snapped. I was going to ask those nearest to make sure he did stay but when I looked at them I didn't see much eagerness to insist on fair play.

That was when Ableman grabbed me by the jacket collar and the left arm. "Come on, you poxy bastard," he was growling. He started to drag me to the top of the spiral stairs. Just for the moment he had me off-balance, trying to run me across the room and throw me down the well.

I went with him a few steps and then I steadied myself and dug my foot in and swung my right all the way round in front of my chest and into his face. It wasn't too damaging by the time it arrived but it stopped him.

He banged me in the back of the neck with his right, still holding on to my sleeve, standing half a step behind me, twisting at my arm to keep me facing in front.

I crouched my shoulder and then rammed my head backwards in the direction of his face.

I felt a bit of a jar but he still held on to my sleeve. I braced myself and whacked down on his ankle and instep with my left heel.

That made him gasp a bit. He let go of my arm. I jumped round and got in two bangs at his face. One got him on the forehead. It felt like punching a brick wall. My hand went numb.

He started swinging and rushing, his head well down, his big arms slicing the air, his jacket flapping. I skipped back and hit something. A table, knocked it over. He charged again, shouting and roaring something diabolical. I had to jump back. I felt my right foot landing on something shaky.

Honest to God. Next thing I'm trying to kick my foot free while dodging the wild bull and when I manage to look down I see I've stepped right into the globe of the world!

Couldn't get it off!

He was diving at me with everything, fists, forehead, knees, feet. I was half-conscious of his mate Aldous trying to creep round the wall to get behind me.

I picked up something from another table, one of these old-fashioned oil lamps with the glass funnel. I rammed it at Ableman. The glass broke on his shiny skull. Blood appeared. I threw the brass part of the lamp at Aldous. It missed him and hit a mirror.

I was kicking and shaking my right foot but the world had me well trapped. To get free of it I had to stamp down with my left foot until the thin leather globe looked like a collapsed football.

Ableman took his hand away from his nut and stared at the blood on his palm.

"You poxy bastard!"

I did a neat side-step and got the table between us. He got his hands under it and tipped it up. Bits and pieces of china smashed on the deck. He tried to ram me against the wall with the table.

I made a grab for Aldous and got him by the hair and an arm. I ran him against the table, face first. He went down with a flabby sort of sound.

Still crashing forward, Ableman hit Aldous with the table and fell over him, losing his balance slowly. I nipped to one side and grabbed something on the mantelpiece.

Nicholas was screaming something from the door to the patio. "Not that," I think it was but I'd already hit Ableman on the back of the skull with the stone statue.

It wasn't stone, actually, it only looked like stone. China by the feel of it, when it broke against Ableman's head bones.

He was up and at me in a flash. Raving for a fight he was.

I kept dodging about the room. More stuff got broken. Nicholas was screaming at us to stop breaking up his lovely room.

281

Abelman got me in a corner and came in swinging. I ducked to one side and had a kick at his legs. He half-fell into the black desk with the china panelling.

It couldn't have been too substantial, I heard something cracking as he came down on it.

"That desk is worth eight thousand pounds!" I heard Nicholas yelling. He tried to drag Ableman away from it. He got a thump in the mouth.

Ableman picked up something round and shiny from the desk and hurled it at my head. A glass paperweight I think, in a situation like that you concentrate on the enemy, everything else is a blur.

I ducked and it smashed into some vases on the mantelpiece. Before he could throw another I rushed in close and started to hammer at his face and then at his belly.

His specs broke. He pulled them off his face and threw them behind him and came at me with his head down. Obviously he thought the bear-hug would polish me off — all this jumping about wasn't doing his lungs any favours.

Reckoning he would be a hard bloke

to shake off I tried to dodge him and tripped over a black box, a hi-fi speaker probably. He dived down on to me and the box cracked up under our weight.

Before he got a grip on me I rammed my mouth against his head and sank my teeth into the nearest bit of skin.

Just below the ear I think.

He let out the most awful yelp and jabbed his big knee up into my Niagaras. I went on biting and struggling to get out from under before the paralysing pain started. I got to my knees and he grabbed me round the middle.

I started to fall again, only this time there didn't seem to be any floor. We were right at the top of the spiral staircase. I went down first, bang bang bang. The sharp edge of each bloody step hit my head and my shoulder blades. I managed to get a grip and scramble upright before I fell off into the downstairs room. He came jumping down at me.

I ducked right down and got a hold of his foot before it crashed into my face. I gave him as much of a twist as I could and he went over — roaring and cursing as he saw the smart rugs rising to meet him.

Once you're tangling with a bloke who's done his whack on the cobbles you either forget you're a decent chap or you end up a decent crippled chap.

I should have booted him but I hesitated.

Bang. He got his fingers into my left eye. It felt like he was trying to pull my face off. My balls were churning in a slow agony and my head was roaring and half the world was a dark red place.

I jabbed my fingers into his face. He caught hold of my jacket and whirled me round and hurled me across the room. I hit one of the eggshell chairs and held on to it.

For a moment it was like being on the playground swings. Then the chain took my whole weight. It came tearing out of the ceiling. Half a yard of plaster came down with it. He came at me through the white dust. Aldous was at the bottom of the stairs, getting ready to join in.

I threw the hi-fi player at Ableman. He couldn't have been seeing too well by then. I got something solid off the mantel-piece and clobbered him on the side of the head. It was a clock. Glass broke and more streaks of blood spread over his skull and face.

He yelled for Aldous to help him and picked up the egg-shell chair and came rushing at me with the chair as a battering ram.

I dived to one side and stuck out my foot. He tripped and went careering into the harpsichord.

It played a few notes but not what you could call a tune. I dived after him and hit him low in the back, in the kidneys.

Hard bastard he was. Instead of collapsing he scrambled round to get a grip of me. This time he wasn't going to let go. I nutted him on the nose and he didn't seem to feel it. I kicked his ankle and kneed his groin and still he held on. I thumped his belly. It was as soft as a sack of frozen pork.

I cannot tell a lie, I began to see myself losing this one. I didn't have time to be scared but I knew the kind of kicking I was due if he got me down.

The next thing Aldous jumped on my

back and tried to dig his fingers into my eyes.

I closed them tight and got my fingers round Ableman's ears and started to twist. At the same time I kept ramming my head backwards. I felt it hitting something hard. The weight eased on my back. I swung Ableman round by the ears.

We danced round the room. A table went. Lamps went. The harpsichord was rammed against the wall. Ableman had to keep dancing round with me or get his ears torn off. I had a kick at Aldous when we passed him kneeling on the floor with his hands to his nose and mouth.

Records were smashed, china was smashed, a copper picture came off the wall. A glass bookcase lost its glass. A standard lamp toppled over and smashed one of the bulls-eye window panes.

Then I dug my heels in and braced myself and then I started to move backwards, dragging Ableman and then letting him go.

He went into the wall head down. He hit the floor and let out a horrible little noise and then just sprawled there making jerky movements with his legs.

Aldous was on his feet, backing away, looking for something to use as a club. He looked terrified.

That was when Lou Nicholas appeared down the stairs. He was holding a piece of shiny wood, a bit of a table maybe. His face was white and almost demented.

"You've ruined my home," he screamed. He hit Aldous on the back with the length of shiny wood, a double-armed swing. Aldous threw up his arms as if he'd been shot. Then he measured his length, gasping and yowling something chronic. Nicholas looked set to smash his head in but I got over there and held his arm. I was panting too much to speak.

Beevers came down the stairs.

"Good God!" he said.

"It was that swine there," Nicholas said, pointing his length of furniture at Ableman, who was still flat out on his face. "He said I'd go to jail if I didn't play along with him. I'm sorry, Phil, it wasn't my idea to drag you into it."

"Is there any hot stuff stashed away?" I managed to ask between gasps.

"I don't know."

I touched Aldous on the ear with my toe. He looked up with the eyes of a cornered rabbit. I drew back my foot to kick his head. "Where's the stuff being kept?" I growled at him.

"I dunno, honest, Tommy done most of it, I — "

I raised my foot. "Don't give me that crap."

"All right, all right, there ain't any stuff — he said it was easier blaggin' money outa you two than smugglin' real stuff. Don't hit me, *please* — "

"Blackmail!" Nicholas snapped. "They started out with two or three loads just to get me implicated — then they told me to drag you in too, Phil — I'm sorry, I thought the money was good so it wasn't as if — Christ, I should have — "

"That's all you got to say to the cops then," I said. I went over for a look at Ableman. His eyes were open but he wasn't seeing much.

"I don't think we should get the police," Beevers said nervously.

I lost my temper.

"Jesus Christ — what bloody more do you want? If you don't get him weighed off now he'll be on your back again soon as he feels better."

Nicholas started poking among the wreckage. Beevers got close to me and muttered, "But what about the note and the other things, we don't want the police — "

"Just don't mention it to the cops. I don't think it's got anything to do with this."

"But how can you be sure? I mean — "

"Leave it to me, Mr Beevers, eh? I'm betting you won't be hearing any more from your friend the joker."

"Look, Jim — "

"Just take it easy, Mr Beevers, okay?"

He nodded gratefully.

"I can't phone the police station," Nicholas said. He held up the remains of a fancy phone, the twin of the one in Beevers's flat. For a moment I though he was going to scream and weep and maybe stamp his elegant foot.

"I tried to save the pinball machine," I said. He gave me a sick look.

Before I could stop him he darted across the room and booted Ableman a full-volley in the guts.

289

The Italian cushion-king came down the stairs, followed by some nervy faces.

Nicholas went to use a neighbour's phone. People stared in horror at Ableman lying there on his side, jerking about in slow-motion agony, his face wet with blood and sick. Then they stared at me.

"Poor Lou," said one woman, surveying the general shambles, "they've broken all his best pieces. Why on earth does he have thugs in his house?"

"He's the thug, missus," I snapped, pointing at Ableman, "I'm — "

"You're a *thug*," she said firmly. "Charles? I want to go now."

Quite a few of them left, giving me nasty looks on their way.

That's Chelsea for you.

15

AS I told Beevers, the police have seen it all before. Your big drama is just another bit of the day's work to them. They don't shock easily.

"You'll get a bit of a splash in the papers — maybe not," I said. "What's it all add up to? A villain takes a couple of businessmen for a ride? A bit of a rough-house at a Chelsea party? Dull murders are only getting three lines these days."

Ableman had been taken to hospital and Aldous was in the cells at Chelsea nick. Beevers, Nicholas and myself had to stay in the nick until about eight o'clock giving statements. The cops seemed a bit bored once they realized there wasn't any big load of real filth waiting to be collared.

"Don't you think I should've told them about the other things?" Beevers said as I was driving him to Regent's Park. Simone had gone home earlier in a cab.

"Why complicate matters, Mr Beevers?"

"You're probably right. Are you coming up for a drink?"

"Not tonight, Mr Beevers, thanks. Listen, I don't really know how to put this — "

"You don't have to, Jim, I'm more than grateful to you, I'll have a cheque made out — "

"I haven't actually done the job yet, have I?"

We were sitting in the Stag outside Inverson Court. It was quite dark.

"Of course, you've done the job — it was Ableman — "

"Maybe. Maybe not."

"But you said — "

"I said not to bother bringing the hoaxes and all that up in front of the police, Mr Beevers, you wouldn't want all that business about Thornton's hit and run coming out, would you? I didn't say it was necessarily Ableman and Aldous behind the other caper. In fact I'm pretty sure it wasn't, Mr Beevers. Not their style, all that subtle stuff. You saw how he decided to deal with me — not exactly psychological warfare, was it?"

"But who was doing it then? I mean, Ableman was capable of thinking up a confidence-trick in the first place, wasn't he?"

"Tell you what, Mr Beevers, why don't you let me work on it a couple of days longer, eh? I might have an idea or two."

"If you've got any suspicions — "

"I'd rather know for sure first — no point in giving anybody a bad name unnecessarily, is there?"

"Well, Jim, I'm in your hands." He turned in his seat to look at me. "You were pretty good back there in Lou's house, Jim, you're a real man in my book."

"Well, I didn't have much option, did I? Pretty obvious he and Aldous were going to hammer me, what else was I going to do but — "

"Don't put yourself down, Jim. I don't mind admitting to the whole world if needs be, Ableman had the fear of death up me. I could never have done what you did, Jim. Any money I give you won't really be enough thanks for getting me out of that mess. I'm not much of a man,

Jim, not really, I'm a physical coward, I don't seem to have many brains when it comes to commonsense matters, I — "

"Come off it, Mr Beevers, you got mixed up in something way out of your line, that's all."

"What would you do if you were me, Jim, tell me honestly."

"Better write to Marjorie Proops about that, Mr Beevers."

"I mean about Lou and the business. I don't really have anybody else I can ask for advice like this — "

"I dunno, Mr Beevers — maybe you'd rest easier at nights if you stuck to furniture."

"You're not still suspicious of Lou, are you? I mean, they got him mixed up in it by blackmail, didn't they?"

"As I say, Mr Beevers, why not let me work on a couple of angles for a few days, then we'll see what's what. All right?"

"Sure you wouldn't like a drink?"

"Thanks, I'm going home for a bath and an early night. I'll be in touch during the week."

"All right, Jim. And thanks again. I mean it."

When I got back to Ravenscourt Park I borrowed a bottle of Dettol from Mrs Nordstrom and gave my face a clean-up and then lay in the bath for well over an hour. I couldn't be bothered listening to the radio, specially not the Sunday-night waffle you get on all channels. A scrap like that pays off in pain later. Bruises and aches and depressing thoughts. Beevers said it was to do with being a real man — to me it felt degrading, like behaving the way animals do.

It had been forced on me, which was some consolation, and I'd come out on top, which was better than the alternative, but it still wasn't anything I would ever boast about, even to myself.

One day I might have grandchildren. What could I tell them I did in my prime? People paid me money to snoop about and get in scraps — smashing up houses, I was one of the best at that?

Grandchildren? Don't you need to have children first? Would a nice woman want to hitch up with a bloke who earned by snooping and scrapping?

I was too tired to read in bed but every time I moved another part of me started aching and woke me up.

Just me, alone in the dark, somewhere far off a faint rumble of London by night, just me and that same old question.

Is *this* the best I'm going to get?

★ ★ ★

Monday morning was grey and damp, just in case two consecutive days of sunshine might turn us all into Italian cushion-designers. By half past ten I'd been to the office, read the circulars, phoned Marshall in Bolton — his girl said he was at a conference in Birmingham — and was heading for Regent's Park by way of Marble Arch and Gloucester Place. I'd passed Christine's door quietly. No situation's so embarrassing it doesn't even out in time.

I pulled in about thirty yards from the Inverson Court entrance and switched off. I didn't exactly know what I was hoping to see but I would know it when I did see it.

Cars came and went but nothing

stopped. I chewed gum. It's a vulgar habit for morons we're always being told by sophisticates — usually the same ones who're filling the ashtray.

Some old men in foreign-cut clothes came along the pavement, Germans or Austrians maybe, browner faces than ours, hands doing a lot of the verbal work, one of them with a walking-stick, just four old guys going nowhere particular in the wrong country.

A spade postman in the grey lounge suit with the metal badge on his lapel dropped an elastic band off a bundle of letters and disappeared into the block I was parked beside. Maybe if they used those rubber bands twice they'd save enough dough to make letters cheap enough for ordinary folk again. It would make the pavements safer for a start.

I was there an hour or so when a taxi stopped outside Inverson Court. The driver went inside, a short bloke in a knitted cardigan. Five minutes later he came back out — followed by Simone in a light-grey flannel suit.

He held the door for her and then the taxi headed off into Park Road and down towards Baker Street. The traffic was very heavy in Baker Street. I got in close behind the taxi, only one car between us.

As tailing jobs go it was a cinch. Straight down Baker Street in short hops between the lights, left into Oxford Street, then right into New Bond Street. She got out at the corner of Maddox Street.

I pulled into the kerb, leaving the engine running. She had a look in a jeweller's window then walked on a few yards and went into a shop. I gave her a couple of minutes then I switched off and released the bonnet and got out.

I left her standing there with the bonnet up. Might fool a teenage warden for half an hour I reckoned.

The shop was a travel agency. Passing the door I had a quick glimpse of her standing at the counter with a man talking to her.

I crossed at the lights and waited on the corner of Grosvenor Street. She was about twenty minutes in the travel agency and when she came out she was putting a white folder in her brown shoulder-bag.

She walked down Bond Street looking

in various windows. Killing time it looked like. She went as far down as Burlington Street and into the Arcade.

She did the whole length in there, looking in all the windows, occasionally looking at her watch. A nice young lady from the country, you might have thought, up in town for a bit of shopping and lunch with an old school friend.

Then she turned and came back towards me, walking a bit quicker.

I dived into the nearest shop and picked up the first thing I saw, a tightly-rolled umbrella as it happens.

"Can I help you, sir?" said the young bloke behind the counter. I kept the back of my head to the window until she'd had time to get past. When I looked out I saw her white-blonde hair moving quickly away up the Arcade.

"Sorry," I said, "I really wanted one with a sword in it."

He frowned but I was gone.

She turned left again towards Bond Street, then right, up the pavement on the east side. She turned into Conduit Street. I saw my bonnet sticking up in the air like a hungry crocodile. I kept about twenty yards behind her, easily following the dash of white-gold among the crowds.

She went into a restaurant, one of these cute little Italian places just a bit too pricey for typist girls with luncheon vouchers.

I hung about on the other side for about five minutes to make sure she was staying in there. I went back to the motor and closed the bonnet and did a fast tour of the streets between Bond Street and Regent Street till I got a meter on the south side of Hanover Square.

Then I nipped back to Conduit Street. I'd lost about ten minutes so they were probably already into the soup course.

She *had* to be meeting somebody. After all that commontion in Partner Lou's dinky little house she would be desperate to talk. And she couldn't risk asking her friend up to Inverson Court.

Lou Nicholas, of course. It had to be. She said she despised and loathed him but that night in the discotheque they'd looked pretty solid with each other.

Lou was being skinned by Ableman but a sharpie like him can always see an angle. Bert Thornton's weird little revenge campaign would have given them the idea — make the hoaxes a bit more dramatic and frighten Beevers into coughing up fifteen grand. Only getting some of her own money back was how she probably saw it.

All I had to do was see them together and I'd be able to tell Beevers his fifteen grand was safe. His marriage would be finished but he could stop sweating.

★ ★ ★

I was hanging about on the opposite pavement when I had one of those thoughts. The sudden flash sort of thought. I was snooping here, wasn't I?

I said the word a few times. *Snooping.* Tell you what I did, kids, when I was in my prime. I was a snooper. I hung about in doorways *snooping* — for money, of course, that's what made it all right.

Say a word like that often enough

301

and it begins to sound like monkey-talk.

★ ★ ★

I went across the street and into the restaurant. An Italian in a red shirt asked me if I had a reservation.

"I'm meeting a friend," I said, peering round the cosy little nooks. "Yeah, there she is."

Coming at her in the dim lighting, with the window at my back, the bloke pulling back my chair, she couldn't see my face too clearly.

"I thought you were never going — "

Then she saw who I was. Her mouth dropped open. "Oh. It's you."

"Who did you think it was?"

"What are you doing here?"

I pulled one of those crusty straws out of the Cellophane packet and broke off an inch or two.

"My office is quite near here," I said. "Small world, innit?"

"I'm meeting a girl friend — you'd better go or she'll tell everybody I'm having an affair."

"You get seven out of ten for quick thinking."

She gave me a cute little smile. Such lovely big healthy teeth. To think my tongue had been all round them. "You know what Philip's like," she said, "if it got back to him we were seen together he would think the worst. *Please.*"

"Don't panic — I'm doing you a favour."

I didn't have to bother watching the door. I kept my eyes on her face. Her eyes kept flicking from me to the door and back again. The Italian shoved a menu in front of me. Would sarr like a dreenk before he ordarrs?

"Yeah, you got any lager in bottles?"

I put my elbows on the table and gave her a smile. "As I say, I'm trying to help you."

"Why should I need your help?"

"We all need help from somebody, don't we? Thing is, I bet he put you up to it, didn't he? So we got to find a way to get you out of it."

"What are you talking about?" Her eyes went to the door. "Oh my God," she muttered. She closed her eyes.

I waited till I sensed him at my back. Then I turned and looked up with a big smile. Wasn't I Jack the Lad to have caught them at it?

Only it wasn't Lou Nicholas staring down at me, it was Paul Shirriff.

16

THE new plastic man didn't even break step.

"I'll sit against the wall," he said to the Italian impresario. "Sorry I'm late, Simone — hello, Jim, I didn't know you used this place. I'll have a dry martini, please."

I broke off another bit of straw.

"He's been following me," she said to him, "now he's going to tell Philip about us."

"What about us?" he said, looking at me airily. "No harm in having a spot of lunch together, is there?"

"Like it," I said.

She went a bit red and looked to him for help. He had a gander at the menu. Without looking up he said, "All right then, let's not be naïve about it. But he didn't hire you to spy on her, did he?"

Some new customers came tramping past. Our friend in the red shirt dropped off our drinks and said he would be back to take our ordarrs in joost a momento.

"He hired me to find the menacing jester," I said. "Looks like I've done it now, dunnit? Must admit though, you're a surprise. I'd have bet money it was Lou Nicholas put her up to it."

"I beg your pardon," he said.

She frowned. "Put me up to what?" she demanded.

I made a cigar out of the rest of the straw. I could have done with a cigarette as it happens but I'd managed a whole day without even one and I wasn't going to spoil the achievement, not just yet anyways.

"We were looking for somebody who knew you both well enough to have access to your keys, Mrs Beevers. Also how he get into the block? Your husband asked the desk to weed out all dodgy callers. The inside stairs? Only that door is locked on the inside. So somebody must've opened it from the inside. Do I have to go through the whole business?"

He shook his head. They looked at each other and shrugged.

"This isn't a light comedy," I snapped,

"at least I don't see the judge finding it too hilarious."

Shirriff leaned across the table and peered into my face. "You don't *look* particularly unbalanced," he said, "and you haven't been drinking — "

"Just listen to what I'm going to tell Mr Beevers," I said, "all right?"

He peered at me again. "Fighting *again* James? Tuts tuts, what an uneven life you lead. Every time we meet your face is showing signs of recent combat. Now if you had a partner with a sense for business — "

"For Christ's sake!" I shook my head. "Just listen, eh? Thornton starts it — just silly stunts at first but then they get more serious because Thornton's done for himself and some other joker has stolen his idea. Who? Somebody who knew Mrs Beevers was at the hairdressers', who had a key, who could get through the locked door to the inside stairs. Who also knew Mrs Beevers is actually twenty-eight, although she thinks twenty-six sounds better. Oh yeah — and he's close enough to slip a dead mouse into her pocket. Shame that, innocent little mouse. So I'm on the scene by then and everybody's telling me what a crude bastard this Manders is and what a diabolical chiseller this Lou Nicholas is. So then I dig up the fact that Mr Beevers has got himself tied up in a porn smuggling racket and he can't readily go to the cops. As it happens the porn racket is another trick being played on poor Mr Beevers — Lou Nicholas and Tommy Ableman are screwing him from the north and the anonymous hoaxer is screwing him from the south, is there anybody who isn't screwing Mr Beevers I wonder."

"Did you know he was in a pornography racket?" he asked her, sounding serious for the first time.

"He told me about it yesterday," she said. She sneered in my direction. "That's where *he* got the bruises on his face, fighting that Ableman person at Lou's house. There's going to be a big court case — as you can imagine Phil is positively *quaking*."

"Go on," I said, "you knew about the porn caper all along."

But the little warning bell was already

tingalinging. They weren't such good actors as that.

"I really don't know what it is you're imagining, James, but let me make our position quite clear. We've been in love for some time. I want Simone to leave Phil and for us to get married after their divorce. Simone won't make up her mind to leave him because she's sorry for him — "

"And also because she's got a lot of her cash tied up in him," I said.

"I don't care about the wretched money," she said angrily, "we'll never get it back now anyway."

Then he smiled!

"James old boy — you may have done us a favour. Yes! Just tell him you caught us holding hands in a Mayfair restaurant and *he'll* start the divorce proceedings. Just the prod Simone needs. Wonderful!"

She and I looked heavily at each other while he was patting his hands together and beaming at us both. Maybe she wanted me to tell him he wasn't the only one doing the dirty on poor old Mr Beevers. Maybe she was just beginning to understand that all this jolly permissive stuff has its snags.

"You'll be poor but happy together, eh?" I said.

"Oh not so poor," he said, "Simone has a few thousand tucked away and I don't exactly work for beer money you know."

"You've got a few thousand tucked away?" I said to her, frowning all over my stupid bruised face. She nodded. "But you put all your money into your husband's business — that's what all this has been about, hasn't it? You know — trying to screw fifteen grand out of him? Come on, stands out a mile — it's got to be — "

But it didn't have to be, did it?

"I told you," she said impatiently, "I got a fifty-thousand pound house in Gerrards Cross as part of the settlement in my divorce — I only gave Philip twenty-five thousand of that. I'm not totally stupid, you know."

"You mean you've got twenty-five thousand left?"

"Less than that now — about twenty thousand I think."

"Oh. Still, you could do with more, couldn't you? Paul here, he likes a good suit and that — "

"What? More from Philip?" she said. "He doesn't have any money."

"Come off it. I know he keeps saying he's broke but — "

"He is broke! He let the furniture business go to pot and there's been hardly any money coming out of Lou Nicholas — the opposite, he's been trying to get me to give him the rest of my money. More working capital he calls it. He's got a hope!"

I frowned. As I say I'm like the weather forecast, bright in patches. Shirriff smiled at me.

"James," he said patiently, "I don't think you're quite *au fait* with these circles. None of them are worth a penny — Simone's the only one with real capital."

"But the flat — the Rolls! And that house of Lou's."

"James, old boy, you're touchingly naïve at times. Philip bought a ninety-nine year lease on the flat years ago, long before inflation. The Rolls is on

311

hire-purchase — through the company. You don't need a lot of money to look rich, James, you only need to know your way around the system."

"Look — that house of Lou Nicholas's — he was screaming at us because we were damaging a bloody desk worth eight grand! Plus all the rest — "

"My dear chap, Nicholas doesn't *own* any of that. It belongs to his mother. She lets him use it while she's in Bermuda with her third husband. I must say, I'd love to be there when she sees the damage."

I could only stare at them. Shirriff gave me a wink. When I next spoke my voice sounded weak even to me.

"But Beevers goes about with a bundle of readies that could rupture a kangaroo — "

"Of course he does. Impressions, James, that's what it's all about. In the final analysis that's all that counts. The real rich don't carry any cash at all, James, the Queen hardly knows what a pound note looks like — "

"But — "

Then my face fell.

If she had the dough and Beevers had

none that meant she had no possible motive for frightening him with all these hoaxes and sick jokes and capers.

So who did have a motive?

Jesus Christ.

"Now I weel take the ordarrs," said the geezer in the red shirt, "Madame would like a try ze calves keedneys, een wine — oooomm."

I pushed back my chair. "Where's your husband likely to be right now?" I said to her.

"In the office if he's not at lunch."

"Are you going?" Shirriff frowned. "Surely we have something to discuss? Are you — "

"I made a big boob," I said, standing up. "Just forget the whole thing."

"But what are you going to tell Philip?" she asked, looking anxious.

"He owes me two grand, that's all I'm going to tell him. See you sometime maybe."

★ ★ ★

I went up to Hanover Square and bunged two bob in the meter. Simple really, you give it money and it gives you time. It doesn't take brains to count minutes.

Maybe they should have pulled a canvas hood over my head. This meter is out of action through illusions that it can think.

One thing was for sure. Next time he brought his big bundle off his hip I wasn't going to be sneering, I was going to be grabbing.

★ ★ ★

I took a taxi to the Aldwych. The entrance was just past the Waldorf Hotel. I took the lift to the third floor. The frosted glass door had *Topaz Artiste Management* painted in black letters.

One step inside and I had a fair idea of where the capital had gone. The big reception room was done up like a whore's heaven, concealed strip lighting for the soft glow look, tables and chairs of glass and steel and black leather, brilliant blue carpeting wall to wall, modern paintings, one wall covered with blow-ups of stars. I didn't recognize any of them but only stars get blown up.

Behind a low glass counter two girls faced each other across a big curved desk. One of them was working an electric typewriter. She was young and fair. The other one was waiting for a call on the red phone or the white phone or the fawn phone. She was young and fair as well, maybe not quite so young or fair.

She got up and came to the counter. She had frizzy curls and a bulging black sweater.

"Can I help you?" she said sweetly.

"Mr Beevers? My name's Hazell."

"That's funny," she said, "you don't look like a Hazel."

I yawned and patted my mouth. "James Hazell if you don't mind, kid."

"Have you an appointment?"

"Just tell him I'm here, eh? Okay?"

She smiled. She had a nice face, small teeth, a slightly upturned nose, a few freckles that didn't look painted on. A bit cheeky looking. "Does he know you?" she said. "You might be somebody he doesn't want to see, mightn't you? If you could tell me what it's about?"

"It's about twenty to two."

One of the white doors on the other side of the big curved desk opened and Beevers stuck his head out. "Angela?" he said, peering and frowning. Then he saw me. "Oh — Jim. Come in."

As I went round behind the glass counter I said to her, "Funny, you do look like an Angela."

"Very tasty," I said as he closed the door. It had Venetian blinds and a big bare desk with nothing on it but a white phone and a red phone, a mounted photograph of Simone, falling backwards over a cliff from the angle of her head, and a mounted slab of clear perspex in the middle of which was an Isle of Man ten bob note. The chair I took was a black leather job with a tubular steel frame. The colour scheme was light grey with bits of purple. The big desk was a rich wine red.

"Like a drink, Jim?" he said, sliding open the glass door of a cabinet set flush into the wall.

"Thanks, bit early for me actually."

He poured himself a glass and showed me the bottle. "Very good malt this, Lou gets it direct from a place in Scotland, not commonly available in pubs down here."

"Tastes better if it's exclusive, does it?"

He grimaced. "I know, Jim, you're dead right, maybe if I met more guys like you I'd cure myself of these silly little habits." He sat down across the desk from me. The slats of the blind were open at the upwards angle, making him a bit shadowy.

"Pretty plush offices you got," I said, "a good front's important I expect."

"Oh yeah, all bullshit in this game, Jim."

"Had any word from the law?"

"Lou's been down at Chelsea police station all morning, I don't know what the score is yet."

"Just stick to your story — Ableman brought in a load of stuff without your knowing and then put the bite on you to play along — you should come out all right."

"How are you feeling anyway, Jim? That was some dust-up you had yesterday — it's going to set Lou back a few quid putting his house back in order."

"It only hurts when I breathe. Won't be able to wear those trousers or jacket again I shouldn't think."

"Put it on your expenses, Jim, I don't want you to lose anything over this, you did more than I could have legitimately expected — "

"Well I was earning my two grand, wasn't I? What's a pair of strides and a jacket and a few aches and pains against that kind of money?"

He nodded briskly. "Jim — soon as you tell me you've wrapped it all up and I'm free of any more hoaxes or practical jokes or threatening letters — you'll have your two thousand. Be a pleasure to give it you."

The phone rang. The white one. He picked it up. "Beevers here," he said. He listened for a bit. "I've got somebody here actually, can I give you a tinkle later on, Harry? Fine." He put down the white phone and picked up the red phone. "Angela? Put a stop on all calls, I'm in conference for the next ten minutes or so. Thanks." He put down the red phone.

"Maybe take longer than ten minutes,

Mr Beevers," I said.

"If we could keep it short, Jim, I'm hoping to see my solicitor later this afternoon, get wheels in motion. We must get rid of these horrible dirty-book shops."

"What about the partnership? Aren't you winding it up?"

He shrugged. "Maybe I was panicking a bit, Jim — I don't *like* what Lou did to me but he didn't really have a lot of choice, did he, not with Ableman on his back? Maybe I'll let it ride for a little while, see how the wind blows. Like a cigar?"

"Very nice."

He brought a flat box of them out of a drawer and came round the desk. I lifted one out, quite a big one it was. He lit me with the gas lighter. I got up and went round the other side of the desk to his big leather chair. "Always wondered how it'd feel, the big tycoon behind the desk," I said, sitting down. He gave me a cheery little nod and a wink.

"That's where the worries are, Jim, that side of the desk."

He had the light on his face now. He

went on smiling, waiting for me to give him his chair back. I blew cigar smoke at the ceiling and put my elbows on the desk.

"Okay then, Mr Beevers, let's get down to the business."

Seeing I was staying put he took the chair I'd been in. "*Have* you dug up anything new?" he asked.

"I wondered why you were so scared in particular about that smashed windscreen at Wembley on Saturday," I said. "Course, I know now — that was the one bit of menacing hoaxing that came as a surprise to you, wasn't it?"

He frowned. He was facing the light now and he had to squint to see what my face was doing. I leaned back and tugged at the string of the Venetian blinds. They closed altogether until I got the hang of it. For a moment the room was almost in darkness and then I got them open as far as they would go. He was still frowning.

"I don't quite follow you, Jim — you said that was probably just some layabout who couldn't get into the game and took his spite out on the nobs with their big cars."

"True enough."

"Well then?"

I had a puff. After a couple of days without a cigarette the cigar was strong enough to make me feel just a bit woozy. I liked the feel of it in my hand but I kept it well away from my mouth.

"You still got that note, Mr Beevers?"

"Yes — why?"

"Could I have a dekko at it?"

He brought it out of his inside jacket pocket. He was wearing a dark grey suit, flannel of course, everything about Philip Beevers was flannel some way or another.

I reached for it across the desk and opened the envelope. I held up the sheet of typed paper. He kept staring at me, still frowning.

"That machine outside I shouldn't wonder," I said, "electric typewriters always look a bit neater than the steam-driven sort."

He let his mouth fall open. "You think it was done *here*? But he wouldn't have been so stupid — the police can match up typewritten stuff as easily as matching fingerprints."

"The cops were never going to see this, were they, Mr Beevers? I was to see it and Mrs Beevers was to see it — but nobody else. You're a clever man really, Mr Beevers, a lot more tricky than I ever gave you credit for. Course — I'm not winning any Brain of Britain contests, am I?"

He shook his head slowly, puzzled, looking to see if I was maybe joking or maybe if I was going off my rocker. "I don't know what you're getting at, Jim."

"No. The only thing that's worrying me is this two grand you're due to bung me, Mr Beevers — I don't reckon you ever had any serious notion of paying me, did you?"

He jumped to his feet. "Look, Jim, I said we'd have to keep this short — are you sure you're not still just a bit groggy from fighting Ableman yesterday? Perhaps you should take a day off, have a rest, we could — "

"Sit down, Mr Beevers. I should've been hit on the head sooner actually."

"Now look, Jim — "

"Now you look, Mr Beevers." I waited

322

till he sat down. I leaned back in the big leather chair. "You'd have made it work — only I'm one of these naïve sorts who does a fair day's graft for a fair day's greens."

That was when another Beevers took over. The puzzled smile went missing. His eyes became bright and determined. He stood up.

"I think you're probably concussed, Jim," he said firmly. "Give me a ring tomorrow or Wednesday, we can discuss this rationally."

"It's going to take two grand to get your chair back, Mr Beevers," I said.

"I'm getting annoyed, Jim!"

"Yeah, I can see."

"Give me that note please."

"Uh huh. You get that thrown in for the two grand."

He started round the desk towards me. I swivelled the big leather chair to face him.

"Don't push me too far, Jim."

"Only as far as two grand, Mr Beevers. We made a deal and I've completed my end of it. Not often the client is also the joker but there you go."

"Get out!" he shouted.

"Sure — when I've got two thousand quid that's owing to me." I stretched out and lifted off the red phone. "This is the line for Angela, isn't it?" I said, holding it towards him. "Better tell her to ring the Chelsea nick, keep it all under the one roof."

"Are you mad, Jim?"

"Who can tell these days?"

I put the phone to my ear. The line was open.

"That you, Angela?" I said, "Mr B would like a word."

He dived for the phone. "Never mind," he snapped, slamming it back on the rest. "Say your piece then, Jim — I presume you have some nonsense you want to tell me."

"Only that I've twigged to you, Mr Beevers."

He sighed impatiently and looked at his big wrist-watch, "I'll give you exactly five minutes," he said. He sat down. I held up the cigar. The ash was thick and black.

"First you couldn't get the cops because, you said, Thornton might be the joker and that might lead the cops to turning up the hit and run. Right? On the other hand, you said, it could be Tony Manders. So I find out it *was* Thornton — at least he got the ball rolling. Poor bastard went off his rocker, sitting there in that little house cursing you for turning him into a criminal. But he committed cash and carry before the serious stuff started. So — all down to Manders we thought. But no — he's a hooligan and a headcase but not in a million years clever enough to think up a scheme like that. Right from the off I had a fair idea it had to be somebody pretty close to you and your wife. The keys, knowing when she would be out, knowing how to get past George Jobsworth at the desk. Oh yeah — he also knew your wife's real age, not her moody age. Then that stunt with the mouse — funny how they were all aimed specifically at your missus, wasn't it? Good thinking that — I'm supposed to think it's got to do with her and not you at all. She's meant to think the same thing. In fact, she's meant to be scared out of her skin. Then we go in the big limousine to Wembley and the windscreen gets smashed. You were really scared then. Makes sense now but at the time I thought it was just the strain beginning to tell."

"That's exactly what it was!"

"So we get back to Inverson Court and there's this note — at last we know the strength of it. Some bastard knows you can't afford to go near the cops and he wants fifteen grand or your wife suffers. So you're bottling it by then and you tell me about the porn set-up. You're scared because you can't understand the windscreen being smashed — you're thinking there's some *other* joker getting in on the act. Must've been worrying for you — no, let me finish then we'll have the debate. You own up to me about Nicholas and the porn deal — I say let's put the whole thing in front of Nicholas because I'm thinking he could fit the bill very well. I didn't tell you everything I was thinking — thought I'd spare your feelings till I was sure."

"Sure of what?"

"I think — ah ha — all these stunts were aimed at your wife to put us off the track. *She* was the one who supplied the key and left the stairs doors open and put the poor little mouse in her own pocket — "

He let me see the whites of his eyes, all the way round. "Jesus Christ, Jim — of course! Simone! Oh my God! You mean, she — "

"Hang about. Remember I said I'd work on it for a couple of days longer because I had a few angles?"

"Yes, you did! Oh Jim — I almost wish you hadn't told me about it. *Simone?* I can understand Lou, the bastard, he's trying to clean me out any way he knows. But *Simone?*"

"Yeah, I was thinking along those lines. So I went to these drops — the lock-up and workshop. No porn — Nicholas is conning you. Great, I'm thinking — I'll win the Sherlock of the Year Award and move up into a better class of business on the strength of the publicity. Only it turns out that Ableman is the moving force there — he's tied up Lou Nicholas and Nicholas is forced to drag you in — maybe not as reluctantly as he's saying now but there you go. So I'm

327

still thinking — not happy with fannying you out of dough with the porn caper Nicholas and your missus are trying to screw another fifteen grand out of you with these nasty little stunts. You're so turtles about her you'll shell out another fifteen grand to keep her safe."

"Exactly what I would have done! *Simone?* Oh God, I feel sick. I love that woman, Jim, I can't tell you — "

The phone rang. The white one. I picked it up. A girl's voice said, "I have a call for you, Mr Beevers — "

"He's feeling sick," I said, "ring him back later, eh?" I put down the white phone. I swivelled the chair round to face him again. "So I decide to tag along behind your wife for a bit, see who she meets — Nicholas I'm expecting."

"Did she — meet him?" For a moment he stopped looking sick. Hope shone from every pore. I shook my head slowly.

"No, she didn't meet Nicholas this morning, Mr Beevers. I followed her to Bond Street. She went into a travel agents' first off — maybe she's planning a holiday? I thought I'd better have it out with her before she got a ticket to

Timbuctoo. That was it, Mr Beevers, that's when it all clicked."

"What did she say?"

"She said you don't have any money, Mr Beevers."

"What? I don't understand."

"Money. Like bread — loot — dough — readies — "

"I don't mean *that*, you fool. Of course I've got money."

I looked round the office. "You got a lot of fancy decor, Mr Beevers, and you got a very swish flat there in Inverson Court — china leopards, the lot. But how much is there *cash*, Mr Beevers, like the ready?" I rubbed my thumb and finger together.

He shrugged and tried to look too important to have checked his bankbook lately.

"Know what I think, Mr Beevers? Should've struck me earlier. When I first met you, last week, you were late because of some big deal, a last-minute phone call from Copenhagen. Then I rang you here and the girl said you were taking a call from Amsterdam. What was all that about? Don't spoil the game, let me guess. You were fixing up to do a bit of porn importing off your own bat, weren't you? A load that Lou Nicholas wasn't going to know about. You've been scheming away quietly — going through his desk at night to dig out his contacts and his drops. It wouldn't surprise me if you've got a big load ready to come into the country in one of your furniture containers. The only snag being you don't have the readies to pay for it over there. Your wife's got money but she's turned very tight, hasn't she? Good touch that, the white mouse. Buy it in the Harrods pet shop, did you?"

He had stopped acting by then.

"You can't prove anything," he said firmly.

"Do I have to?"

"What do you imagine you're going to do?"

"I imagine I'm going to pick up what's owing to me under our arrangement and then walk out of here, Mr Beevers."

He got to his feet and went to the drinks cupboard. I knew what was going on under that dyed black hair. Wriggle wriggle.

He turned with a sneer on his face. "You can piss off, Jim," he said, "there's no way I'm paying you two thousand. Tell Simone this cock and bull story if you like — she's going to rush to the cops and accuse me of demanding money with menaces? No way, Jim."

"I was hoping you wouldn't put it like that, Mr Beevers." I swung my feet up on to the nice big shiny desk.

"You'd better leave right now — "

"I hate sounding like a shit, Mr Beevers, but we made a deal. Two grand. Any other time I might've felt a bit sorry for you but I'm being evicted from my flat and I'll need to be paying for a new place. If I tell your wife I think she will make a fuss, you see I didn't nab her with Lou Nicholas, I came across her with that other dear and mahvellous friend of yours Paul Shirriff. He reckons she's leaving you to marry him, Mr Beevers. She's hesitating because she's sorry for you — at least that's what she's telling him. When she realizes you were the anonymous joker I think she'll stop hesitating, don't you? You want it all out in the divorce case? How you terrorized your sweet young wife — having already had twenty-five grand off her? And if that isn't enough — you want me to tell the cops about these calls of yours to Copenhagen and Amsterdam?"

"You wouldn't — "

"As I say, I hate myself for sounding like a shit, Mr Beevers, but we did make a deal, two grand if I got you out of this mess. I had to fight Manders, I had to break into locked premises, I could've been kicked into the plastic surgery ward by Ableman — but in the end I came up with the answer. Sorry — you give me what's owing or I'm afraid I'm dropping you right in it."

He closed his eyes. He did a bit of moaning and swallowing. "Is that true about Simone and Paul?" he muttered through the birth of a sob. I nodded.

He flopped down in the other chair and started to weep. His big body shuddered with pain and anguish.

Don't be soft, Jim, I told myself, it's only acting.

He looked up. His face was wet and red. He was breathing in terrible spasms.

His big sad eyes begged me for sympathy and help.

I put the cold cigar between my teeth. I didn't owe him *anything*. He'd used me all along, dragged me in to keep Simone from calling the police, given me a few quid to go through the motions, picked me for a gorblimey dumbo who couldn't detect gas with his head in the oven.

No, here was where I joined the winners or the losers. I cannot tell a lie, I hated myself. The poor, fat, pathetic twit. Every smiling face in vision had been screwing him and I was as near to a friend as he could buy — and what was I doing?

Destroying him — no other word for it.

Just as I was going to join the losers he straightened up and wiped his eyes. "All right, Jim," he said, "two thousand was what I said."

He brought a thin leather folder out of his jacket pocket. He flattened it on the desk and got out a pen.

"You want it made out to cash?" he said. "It's all right, Jim, there's enough to cover it. I won't try to stop the cheque."

Funny about forcing yourself to act the shit.

It gets easier with practice.

"How much cash have you got on you?" I said.

His right hand dived for his hip. Out came that familiar big bundle. He threw it across the desk at me.

I counted it methodically. It came to seven hundred and eighty-two pounds.

"Yeah, make the cheque out for the balance," I said, "what's that then? One thousand, two hundred and — never been good with figures myself."

"One thousand, two hundred and eighteen pounds."

"Yeah well, you're the big financial wizard, aren't you?"

He slid the cheque across the table.

I shoved the bundle in my hip pocket. I looked at the cheque.

"Is that all?" he said.

"I'll send you a receipt."

I got up and went round the desk.

"Why did you do it anyway?" I said.

He shrugged, still sitting there on the wrong side of his tycoon's desk. "I thought Simone was planning to leave me — for Lou actually. I didn't see why he should get her money. She's a very mean person, you know. With money anyway."

"Maybe you should take a lesson from her."

"Jim — you're right. I did hire you because Paul told me you were keen but thick — I couldn't let Simone call in the police but I had to make some sort of show. Paul was wrong, Jim. You're not stupid, Jim. I'm sorry for having tried to con you."

"That's all right, happens all the time. Here — you did give Bert Thornton five grand — I wouldn't want you to think everybody in this world is trying to clean you out completely."

I tore the cheque in half and dropped it on the desk.

He was still sitting there when I closed the door.

17

AS it happened Beevers didn't have to go through the publicity of Ableman's trial. That came later, long after it mattered to him.

I heard about it on the Wednesday. I thought I should give it a couple of days before I rang the girl, it's never wise to let them think you're panting.

"Oh hallo," I said when she answered the phone, "I'm the one who doesn't look like a Hazel. I suppose a drink tonight or a bite to eat would be out of the question."

"Why do you think so?" said Angela, the one who wasn't quite so fair or so young as the other one. "Isn't it shocking about Mr Beevers?"

"Oh — you've heard. Tell you himself, did he?"

"Pardon? How could he tell me? He fell off the balcony of his flat last night. He didn't tell me he was going to do it."

"What? Is he — dead?"

"Yes, the porter found him this morning. The police have been here asking questions. Did you know that Mrs Beevers left him — she walked out on him yesterday. They said he must have been drinking an awful lot on his own."

"Jesus."

"It's horrible. I quite liked him as a boss actually. Where were you thinking of taking me tonight? I live in Loughton, it's difficult about getting home — unless you've got a car I'll have to catch the last tube. Not that I make a habit of dating any stray man who . . . "

★ ★ ★

Taught me a few things that job. Trust nobody, not even the client. Specially not the client.

And was I glad I tore up his cheque?

Imagine if it had been going through the bank while he was dead. Talk about stealing the pennies off the eyes of a corpse!

Still, I didn't do too badly. I did end

up with the big bundle from his hip
— only I bunged it straight in the bank.
Simone was right — there was a time
back there when I was letting all these
rich bastards make me jealous. Not very
manly, is it?

I did treat myself to a pair of hand-
made saint loueys from a swish shoe-shop
in Bond Street. Cost fifty-eight quid!

Not all that, are they?

THE END

Other titles in the
Ulverscroft Large Print Series:

TO FIGHT THE WILD
Rod Ansell and Rachel Percy

Lost in uncharted Australian bush, Rod Ansell survived by hunting and trapping wild animals, improvising shelter and using all the bushman's skills he knew.

COROMANDEL
Pat Barr

India in the 1830s is a hot, uncomfortable place, where the East India Company still rules. Amelia and her new husband find themselves caught up in the animosities which seethe between the old order and the new.

THE SMALL PARTY
Lillian Beckwith

A frightening journey to safety begins for Ruth and her small party as their island is caught up in the dangers of armed insurrection.

THE WILDERNESS WALK
Sheila Bishop

Stifling unpleasant memories of a misbegotten romance in Cleave with Lord Francis Aubrey, Lavinia goes on holiday there with her sister. The two women are thrust into a romantic intrigue involving none other than Lord Francis.

THE RELUCTANT GUEST
Rosalind Brett

Ann Calvert went to spend a month on a South African farm with Theo Borland and his sister. They both proved to be different from her first idea of them, and there was Storr Peterson — the most disturbing man she had ever met.

ONE ENCHANTED SUMMER
Anne Tedlock Brooks

A tale of mystery and romance and a girl who found both during one enchanted summer.

CLOUD OVER MALVERTON
Nancy Buckingham

Dulcie soon realises that something is seriously wrong at Malverton, and when violence strikes she is horrified to find herself under suspicion of murder.

AFTER THOUGHTS
Max Bygraves

The Cockney entertainer tells stories of his East End childhood, of his RAF days, and his post-war showbusiness successes and friendships with fellow comedians.

MOONLIGHT
AND MARCH ROSES
D. Y. Cameron

Lynn's search to trace a missing girl takes her to Spain, where she meets Clive Hendon. While untangling the situation, she untangles her emotions and decides on her own future.

NURSE ALICE IN LOVE
Theresa Charles

Accepting the post of nurse to little Fernie Sherrod, Alice Everton could not guess at the romance, suspense and danger which lay ahead at the Sherrod's isolated estate.

POIROT INVESTIGATES
Agatha Christie

Two things bind these eleven stories together — the brilliance and uncanny skill of the diminutive Belgian detective, and the stupidity of his Watson-like partner, Captain Hastings.

LET LOOSE THE TIGERS
Josephine Cox

Queenie promised to find the long-lost son of the frail, elderly murderess, Hannah Jason. But her enquiries threatened to unlock the cage where crucial secrets had long been held captive.

THE TWILIGHT MAN
Frank Gruber

Jim Rand lives alone in the California desert awaiting death. Into his hermit existence comes a teenage girl who blows both his past and his brief future wide open.

DOG IN THE DARK
Gerald Hammond

Jim Cunningham breeds and trains gun dogs, and his antagonism towards the devotees of show spaniels earns him many enemies. So when one of them is found murdered, the police are on his doorstep within hours.

THE RED KNIGHT
Geoffrey Moxon

When he finds himself a pawn on the chessboard of international espionage with his family in constant danger, Guy Trent becomes embroiled in moves and countermoves which may mean life or death for Western scientists.

TIGER TIGER
Frank Ryan

A young man involved in drugs is found murdered. This is the first event which will draw Detective Inspector Sandy Woodings into a whirlpool of murder and deceit.

CAROLINE MINUSCULE
Andrew Taylor

Caroline Minuscule, a medieval script, is the first clue to the whereabouts of a cache of diamonds. The search becomes a deadly kind of fairy story in which several murders have an other-worldly quality.

LONG CHAIN OF DEATH
Sarah Wolf

During the Second World War four American teenagers from the same town join the Army together. Forty-two years later, the son of one of the soldiers realises that someone is systematically wiping out the families of the four men.

THE LISTERDALE MYSTERY
Agatha Christie

Twelve short stories ranging from the light-hearted to the macabre, diverse mysteries ingeniously and plausibly contrived and convincingly unravelled.

TO BE LOVED
Lynne Collins

Andrew married the woman he had always loved despite the knowledge that Sarah married him for reasons of her own. So much heartache could have been avoided if only he had known how vital it was to be loved.

ACCUSED NURSE
Jane Converse

Paula found herself accused of a crime which could cost her her job, her nurse's reputation, and even the man she loved, unless the truth came to light.

BUTTERFLY MONTANE
Dorothy Cork

Parma had come to New Guinea to marry Alec Rivers, but she found him completely disinterested and that overbearing Pierce Adams getting entirely the wrong idea about her.

HONOURABLE FRIENDS
Janet Daley

Priscilla Burford is happily married when she meets Junior Environment Minister Alistair Thurston. Inevitably, sexual obsession and political necessity collide.

WANDERING MINSTRELS
Mary Delorme

Stella Wade's career as a concert pianist might have been ruined by the rudeness of a famous conductor, so it seemed to her agent and benefactor. Even Sir Nicholas fails to see the possibilities when John Tallis falls deeply in love with Stella.